WHERE THE LIGHT STOPS DEAD

MR. MICHAEL SQUID

VELOX BOOKS
Published by arrangement with the author.

Cover art by Mr. Michael Squid.

CONTENTS

"Last night I saw upon the stair a little man who
wasn't there…"
—William Hughes Mearns, Antigonish

INTRODUCTION

This is a collection of continually growing horror stories. All are horror, the one genre I've craved a visceral response from in reading and watching since I was a child. I hope to share that skin-crawling feeling of pure fear with you. Thanks to the No Sleep and Short Scary Stories communities and all of the talented authors there and elsewhere for inspiring and challenging me, and thanks to everyone who helped edit and spot errors.

Most of all, thanks to all of the readers, and those sharing compliments and constructive criticism. Thank you for keeping me afloat through very dark times with your invaluable support. I hope I can horrify you and elicit the chills I crave that drove me to create these stories in the first place.

OCCUPIED

We'd finished a modest pasta dinner with salad and I was looking forward to catching up on some shows I'd been watching. I scrubbed the dishes, then loaded the dishwasher, drying my hands with a coarse rag before walking to the bathroom door to find it shut. A light knock returned my father's deep voice, "Occupied," so I headed to the living room and passed some time with a puzzle game on my phone, sunk into the couch. I completed a few levels as my mother worked through a stack of legal documents in the study, when my nagging bladder led me once more to the bathroom door, still closed. "Hurry up dad," I pleaded.

He returned a deep, muffled cough then, "Give me a minute."

I looked at my phone's clock and realized he must have been in there at least half an hour already. I explained this through the door to the answer of "My stomach is just a little upset, I need a minute."

Something started to feel very wrong. Perhaps it was the lack of humor in his voice, devoid of his usual grumpy tone, or perhaps it was the fact he'd had an operation just last year and he now seemed more mortal, more fragile than before. "I'm using yours then," I snapped to no response. I walked through my mother's study to inform her but she wasn't there. I headed up the stairs to find their room empty, their bathroom door closed as well. I knocked on the door only to hear my mother's deadpan response: "Occupied." I wondered if and how food poisoning could be the culprit, and since I merely needed to go number one, I headed out the back door and relieved myself behind a bush. I felt a little exposed in the night's breeze, but at least the view was blocked from any neighbor's homes. I returned inside to my room to watch some TV and tried to forget about it.

Two episodes later, I had a nagging feeling of unease and checked the bathroom door and found it still locked shut. "Dad, what's going on? Can I get you anything?" I asked, my tone laced with concern.

"I'm fine, just give me a minute," he responded in the same lackluster voice. I looked at my phone, it had been two hours. Something was very wrong. I raced upstairs to my parents' bedroom, to their bathroom door.

"Mom, what's going on? Are you OK?" I called frantically. "I'm fine, just give me a minute," she said, the exact words. "It's been two hours!

Something is clearly wrong!" I barked, unable to mask my concern.

"Just a sec," she responded. I thought I heard something, perhaps electrical or insect, something buzzing or scraping, but it was barely audible and gone quickly. I headed back, defeated, to my room and resumed my show.

I must have dozed off. When my eyes stretched open it was daytime, and my cell read 10:45. I trudged a zombie-like shuffle to the bathroom and twisted the handle, locked. Dread welled in my stomach as I remembered the night before, and I knocked on the door.

"Occupied," my dad's voice called back and then I heard it, the muffled sound similar to cicadas, but much softer and lower in tone. I sniffed, fighting the urge to cry, then noticed the odor. It wasn't a septic one, it was the sour stench of a dead mouse swept from behind a fridge, the foul odor of decay when stumbling upon half of a deer in the woods.

I twisted the handle and said, "Dad, I'm very worried about you, just open the door." There was a low, phlegm-filled cough followed by a baritone, vibratory response, "Give me a minute." I raced upstairs, my parents' bathroom door locked as well. My mother's voice, "Give me a minute," repeated like a script when I knocked. Dozens of flies circled the bedroom, buzzing and hovering past my batting hands. I removed my phone with shaky fingers and I dialed 911, not yet pressing send.

"Open the door now or I'm calling 911," I demanded. No response; I dialed. I explained I was worried, that my parents hadn't left the bathroom in over ten hours, that something was very wrong. After some convincing, they agreed to send an officer, and I waited downstairs on the couch. I opened the doors and windows to air out that rancid smell which was permeating the house, but more flies just kept coming in.

After roughly an hour I heard the car engine and walked outside to meet the officers. I led them inside, over to the bathroom door and the taller officer knocked, saying "I'm a police officer, your son called me because he's concerned, can you please open the door?" to the responding sound of the toilet flushing. He tried the door handle, finding it locked. "Please open the door now or we'll be forced to open it." Nothing. He looked over at the other officer, who nodded, a solemn frown fixed on his face. The tall officer removed a tool and forced the lock, opened the door and immediately buried his face in the crook of his elbow. "My god," he said quietly, coughing violently then gagging.

What was left of my parents' bodies was removed as I sat in the back of a cop car. I wasn't a suspect, they had clarified. They just had a lot of questions about my story, as to why I hadn't called earlier. They explained as gently as possible the bodies had begun to liquefy from decomposition, a stage of decay that usually happens nearly a month after death. They said they are trying to find the cause through toxicology tests. In the meantime I've been staying with my uncle nearby, who's been very helpful through the ordeal that's haunted me and plagued me with despair. His house is much smaller. It has only one bathroom that he entered over an hour ago after dinner. Panic has been coursing through my blood. I knocked on that door a few minutes ago and asked if he was OK. The response was that single ominous word that melted my insides: "Occupied," followed by that faint rattling sound as I tearfully asked, "By what?"

MY WALL SOCKETS BREATHE

I noticed it a few days ago when plugging my new laptop into the electrical outlet on the wall. Warm air rippled over the tiny hairs on my knuckles. I quickly retracted my hand in disbelief and stared at the pair of sockets near the floor. I approached again and placed my hand in front of the slots once more, feeling the warm air breathe in building and waning gusts, the same as you'd feel if you were to breathe on your own fingers. I immediately freaked out and looked online to find no related inquiries aside from slow leaking cold air from outside, which this was clearly not. I grew concerned at the phenomenon and tried to understand what exactly was causing it.

I've lived in this old apartment building no more than six months with my daughter Mabel. She has some minor social developmental disabilities and is apparently on the spectrum, so I wanted her to be near some good schools and resources. That search led us from the Bronx to Manhattan and into this building, which is over a century old and rich with history. The heater clangs at night and can't be adjusted, and the carpet looks unchanged as if flappers from the 20s spilled wine on it, but it is safe, surprisingly affordable, and just large enough for the both of us. At least it felt safe until Monday when I felt the wall sockets breathe.

I took out my screwdriver set and unscrewed the outlet cover, removing the plugs and attached wiring. I was disturbed to see the blackness of a hollowed out back from the rusted metal housing. I used my penlight to shine inside, following the wires back a few inches to an ancient brick wall. I felt a shiver, playing with the idea of someone living within the space, but I quickly talked myself out of it. It was only four inches deep, there was no possible way anyone could fit back there. I soon calmed myself down, taped up the back and returned the plugs and housing into the square cut in the wall and screwed the outlet back securely in place.

I thought not much of it until last night, when I was forcing myself to stay awake in my chair, building spreadsheets on my laptop with some take home work I was trying to wrap up before the holidays.

Mabel was playing with her doll on the carpet, making "Queenie" kiss a plastic horse toy which was too adorable, when she yelled "MY TURN," causing my head to turn and look to see what the commotion was about. Mabel was facing the old heat register grate on the floor, her horse doll missing from view. I asked her where it was and she replied with a flustered sigh, "The room took it back, but it's MY turn to have him." I pulled her away from the grate and asked her what she meant, fear forcing my eyes wide.

"It let me play with the horse toy but it took him away. It isn't fair," she said, pouting, and I then realized I had no recollection of her owning anything like the horse I'd seen. I fetched my light and approached the grate, staring down in absolute horror at the sight of a wide eye staring back from within before sliding quickly out of view.

My heart stuttered and pure fear chilled my spine at the realization that someone or something was inside of the tiny crawl space surrounding the apartment. I raced to my cell on the counter and called my neighbor, Mrs. Benson, nearly shaking with anxiety while hugging my daughter close and trying to sound calm. I asked if we could stop by and, when she agreed, I ushered Mabel out, locked the apartment door with shaky hands, and we walked briskly down the hall to our sweet neighbor two doors down.

Mrs. Benson's door opened, revealing that dyed orange hair puffed up above her wrinkled, smiling face. "I was the most intoxicating actress in the Sixties, but that was another life," she would often say before retelling yarns of one of her rendezvous with celebrities and singers, including Mr. Presley himself. She saw the worried look in my wide eyes and welcomed us in for tea. I only realized once the teacup and saucer were on my lap that my leg was tapping nervously, and I whispered to her I saw something in the floor, in the walls. I expected her to look at me like a lunatic, but she just smiled and nodded, her languid gaze drifting over to her large, framed Picasso reproduction. "I used to call her Clara, after my sister, but I don't think she has a name, and I'd be lying if I had any proof she's a she," Mrs. Benson said with a relaxed smile. "She was here when I moved in back in the early 60s, I found out about her when the rodents almost became a problem." I sat in absolute awe and amazement as she explained.

"Years ago, this part of town was filled with filth. Junkies and drunks, muggers and gangs and everything in between. It was also filled with garbage which attracted smaller pests, roaches and rats." *Still has a fair share of those*, I thought to myself, but I just nodded and let her continue. "I hated rats, so after finally seeing one, I put down a wooden trap. I heard the snap and went to clean it up, but the rat was gone, just a few red drops on the trap. This happened for a few weeks, and I just assumed they somehow escaped, until one day the landlord decided to raise the rent." I stared at her, bewildered and contemplating moving or heading to a hotel to stay the night, but I listened, enthralled as her story continued.

"The landlord was a horrible man, Jerry the Jerk is what I called him as soon as he left my sight, threatening to raise the rent and always eyeing me up and down like that." Mrs. Benson lowered her gaze to my Mabel, her eyes lighting up and a smile spread wide on her face. "Mabel, can you fetch me some tissues from the bathroom?" she asked in a warm-hearted manner.

"Yes, Mrs. Benson," Mabel replied, the most polite little lady, before walking over to give us the privacy Mrs. Benson had been seeking.

"That Jerry barged in and tried to raise the rent one day to an amount he absolutely knew I couldn't pay, offering some lewd suggestion of payment plans. I could tell by the slimy look on his sweaty face he strictly intended for me to make it up to him by other means." I frowned, feeling pity for her plight. She continued in her calm, plodding tone, "I refused to pay or do anything of the sort and said I was leaving at the end of the month, but Jerry refused to hear it. He grabbed me, ripping my dress, and I backed into the wall, pinned by that monster. He was too strong for me to fight him off. I screamed only once before Clara showed up."

Mrs. Benson lifted herself slowly on shaky arms and walked over to the large painting on her wall that I just then realized might not be a reproduction. She tilted the painting diagonally, revealing a large hole in the plaster and splintered wood about three feet in diameter, clearly cracked outward from the inside. I saw black specks of what I assumed to be ancient blood drip from the edges of the hole. Mrs. Benson quickly lowered the painting back in place as Mabel emerged from the bathroom with a box of tissues, and she gently tussled Mabel's silken hair. "Jerry never came back, but his brother Merv was far nicer once he finally showed up to request the newly discounted rent," Mrs. Benson concluded casually. My jaw hung slightly open, fascination outweighing the fear that previously consumed me.

I decided to stay. As insane as it may sound, I feel safer knowing something is looking after. I'm always careful when nailing up paintings, gently tapping a few warning alerts to the enigma that is "Clara" to shift away from an incoming foreign object. I sometimes hear that soft breathing, coming impossibly from multiple sides of the room at once, but I have no desire to find out what Clara exactly is. I can tell she shares toys such as that familiar plastic horse with other children in the building, like Mabel's friend Josephine who lives upstairs.

I occasionally get a glimpse of an eyeball in the grate or in a pipe, and I can now even tell whether the tapping is the ductwork expanding or something more organic, but I've decided to stay. Mabel seems happy to have a babysitter and be part of a unique toy share program as well, and the building is in a great area, close to her classes.

If you listen closely, you may find that my wall sockets breathe, but it's safe, surprisingly affordable, and just large enough for the three of us.

AGGRESSIVE DEER ATTACKS REPORTED

Multiple reports of aggressive deer in separate attacks on pets and owners in the Tri-state area.

The alert was surely peculiar, but I returned to peddling, huffing in steady rhythm on my ride.

I'd been cruising my bike along the Delaware canal towpath, a quaint walking and biking route that was once used for horses to tow boats and barges back in the 1800s. After becoming obsolete, the National Recreation Trail System held onto the gem, giving residents from here and afar a lovely trail to travel the border of New Jersey and PA while immersed in nature. I loved the area and the gradients of fall hues it achieved, as did my adoptive parents long before I joined them as a baby. Mom was infertile and my birth parents passed away in a car accident when I was just a month old.

On my rides, I often see river otters in the canal, ducks and rabbits and of course the timid deer staring in cautious glances from within the woods. They make everything trivial in my life seem just that, and I can connect with nature in a meditative way that makes me feel a part of the world, something my desk job does not do in the least.

A few nights a week I ride the path, waving to other bicyclists and jogging couples with their Chocolate Labs and Cocker Spaniels until the sun sets and I can pop over the Lumberville bridge for a bite at a restaurant on the Jersey side. Tuesday was no different, and a terrible argument with my employer left me in need of some peace.

***

Residents of the Tri-state area have reported pet injuries and a few families report being attacked when exiting their car in Pennsylvania.

I should wear a helmet and I should have proper reflectors, but I do have a handlebar mounted LED that lit the path as the sun sunk behind the shadows of the trees in the fiery hues of a romantic era painting. I crossed the bridge into New Jersey, feeling the burn of my calf and thigh muscles and pushed on, slowing to take a breather on Quarry road where a parking lot is carved from the woodland. There were a few deer gathered in a small huddle, and I slowly got off my bike and took my camera out to capture the shot. It was beautiful and serene in the dimming light, but my camera flash was on, lighting the scene to my frustration. I expected them to bound rapidly away, but they just turned and stared at me.

I looked at the camera's digital menu, amazed to have a second opportunity to take the photo. I truly detested my day job beyond anything, and being an amateur nature photographer had earned me a few small stars in the online community so far; my dream was to pursue it full time someday. I switched the flash off, raised the camera, and snapped a few shots. Looking through the viewfinder, I finally saw the crumpled form of a body on the ground at the hooved feet, red and picked apart.

I lowered the camera in shock, raised it again to look through the viewfinder to verify it was a human, which she clearly was. Her auburn hair had strands yanked out to reveal scalp and skull, the face chewed into a grizzly textured mess, but it was clearly the form of an adult woman the does were feasting on. I capped the lens and slung the camera back and walked to the bike when I heard a squeal from one of the doe that rattled me.

It was like a squeaky door closing, followed by a vibratory snort, and the five deer raised their heads and began walking towards me on spindly legs, twitching their ears with interest. I stepped backwards and, as I quickened my pace, they followed suit, starting to trot after me.

I yelled and shook my arms, but they just kept advancing towards me. I threw a fistful of pebbles hard in their direction, but that only caused them to charge directly at me, and I raced to escape. I jumped on my bike and sped off faster than I'd ever peddled back onto the bridge.

I pedaled fast under the dimming dark blue of the sky. My LED light lit up multiple pairs of white, glowing orbs of eyes in the woods.

Snorts and trots, pounding hooves thumped the ground in pursuit as panic screamed in my brain. My emergency alerts kept vibrating my phone and blaring that awful tone, drawing the attention of those things in the blackening shadows of the trees, but I couldn't slow to silence it.

I just had a few miles to go, but when I finally pulled off into the back parking lot of the local bar restaurant, cars with shattered windshields signaled I wasn't out of danger.

I slowed the bike to a stop, observing a six-point buck smashed through the windshield of a car in the parking lot. I slowly approached, seeing the mess of blood covering the driver, an antler cleanly jutting into his eye socket; both dead. The sky was fully dark, and I ran to the restaurant's dark window to look inside, but it was clearly closed. I pulled out my phone to read an alert.

Fatality purportedly due to an attack on a driver near Delaware Canal. Residents advised to stay indoors until further investigation, press announcement to be given shortly.

I closed the alert, but more kept popping up. I dialed 911 to hear a busy signal, and I heard that horrible high-pitched squeal echo throughout the small residential street nearby. I raced back onto my bike and began peddling vigorously down PA-32, darting my eyes to the left and right. I heard a man screaming and slowed to see a flanneled, gray-haired gentleman I knew backed against his house, two does approaching him, heads low. I was looking around for an improvised weapon when a sickening crack raised my eyes back to the sight of the does bucking his head repeatedly with their rear hooves, flecking the siding of the house with red spots. The man's head caved inward and his body sunk before the does began crunching down loudly on his opened face. I sped off on my bike as soon as I noticed the eyes again surrounding me in the shadows.

Both sides of the street looked like a layered cosmos of stars with the glowing eyes of the woodland creatures who watched me, waiting for me to slow. My legs burned as if searing acid had been injected throughout my muscles as I cycled north, following the river.

The temperature had plummeted and my teeth chattered with each lung-burning breath as I rode in the empty darkness of night, watched by those endless sets of eyes in the woods. Each time I slowed, they advanced, and I pushed my body to unknown limits as I every crank of my pedals boiled down to survival.

In a delirious state of exhaustion, my mind created surreal games and fear as I traversed miles of road through infinite night. I counted road signs and diminishing pairs of glowing eyes until the sun finally made me squint. I'd been riding while half-asleep for the past few miles. Children were being walked to a school bus in a suburban town I only realized was Scranton when I collapsed on the street. I didn't wake up until the nurse at my side greeted me and asked if I knew my name or where I was.

Nature is beautiful until it is terrifying. The will to survive is exemplary in our own story but horrifying if on the page of another's book. It's yet unknown what sent the deer into a fury or if pollutants in the river were to blame for the abnormal behavior, but rabies has been excluded. The dozen families who've lost loved ones need answers, but none exist as of yet. All we can do in the meantime is be aware of the woods, and please try not to feed the deer.

LATE BLOOMER

I first saw them in the square plots by the side of the road, filling me with a whimsical excitement. I'd strolled out of the house and was greeted by a panoply of colors. The smell of honeysuckle and lilac danced in the air, and I noticed the pink, white, and yellow hues of new flowers growing where sickly trees in dusty soil once stood. I thought the agricultural committee had decided to spruce up the town, and I adored it.

The flowers appeared on the local news, and it was soon apparent they were not planted by the board but what the anchor speculated to be "guerrilla gardeners". Though technically illegal, it was clear the whole town was happy with the improvement. A week later, we began to notice flowers in peculiar places.

Tufts of petals sprung from the sewer grates and rain gutters.

Blessings of latticed roots and perennial accents decorated most of our once dreary homes. I'd soon see them sprouting from the lips of manhole covers and drainage ditches. Aside from a few murmurs, nobody seemed too concerned until the plumbing became affected.

News reports drew attention to over a dozen homes suffering from clogged pipes. Footage showed brilliant-hued tulips and buttery daffodils forming bouquets in sink faucets and toilet bowl vases. Those interviewed scratched their heads and displayed 5 liter jugs of weed killer, dismayed that their homes were quickly becoming overtaken.

Photos surfaced of refrigerators completely overrun by the exquisite spectrum of flowers that had grown over every item within.

I began seeing cars swathed in colorful clusters of flowery growth, spilling from gas tanks and wrapping over steel like ornate floats from a parade. Soon, blooming patches covered each square of the sidewalks, sprawling out over lawns and into the street itself. The third week in, I woke in the dead of night from an anguished cry. I opened the window and brushed aside the flowers to witness a living bouquet stagger and collapse still in the street. It took a while to comprehend it was a deer, covered from hooves to antlers in pastel flowers.

We then understood the danger, but by then it was too late. We watched in fear as footage hit the news. Eyelids with unmistakable, flowery clusters spilling out from within. Delicate petals blossoming from ears and throats of patients wheezing their last breaths. The death count began to rise, and many scurried to evacuate, but the burgeoning flowery growth wasn't unique to our town. It was worldwide.

Every surface of my home is now blanketed with lush flowers.

My neighbors' screams muffled into gurgles before fading into silence as they became flower beds. The fragrance of orchids nearly masks their decomposition. I knew from the silence I outlived them all, but today I felt that tickle in my sinus. I saw the tiny, green bud inside my nostril and realized in horror I'm not immune like I'd hoped. I'm just a late bloomer.

BULL #5825

A tasty burger is often found next to a cold beer with friends or with a side fries on a much needed lunch break. They are wholehearted meals, a cheap yet filling reward, and they have become an American staple. I work in a meat packing plant upstate and I enjoy a good burger myself, but the wholesome nature of the burger is long gone for me. I'll spare the details of the slaughterhouse. You can read about them elsewhere online if truly interested. This is a story about mutation; the unstoppable will to survive.

Mutations at the farms were seen on occasion based on the sheer number of animals, though usually just crippling them and preventing them from being suitable for consumption. We had seen a few albino calves, a few extra-limbed cows, we had even seen a cyclops calf with one large orb in the middle of its head one time. All of the mutations I'd seen were detrimental except one that looked like a bodybuilder, and that beast looked strong. I looked it up; it lacked muscle-inhibiting hormone myostatin, a trait that's now actively bred for more muscle mass. This story isn't about any of them, however.

This story is about the bull whose ear was tagged #5825.

He was an Angus beef bull, likely around 17 months old when I started. I'd seen him on the farm we dealt with on one of the trips I helped the boss with. He was a large, dark brown wall of muscle and fat with little or no personality as far as I could tell. He did, however, have a distinctive marking, a single patch of fur on his forehead shaped like a sloppy "S". Some of the other cattle liked being patted or scratched behind the ears, and on those rare visits, I enjoyed giving them some comfort in their time on this planet. Not 5825 however; he seemed emotionally unavailable. He just stared dead to the horizon as if he could somehow sense what followed; the trip to our plant and the machine. He almost looked to be brooding, plotting, but I know I may just be thinking that now, after seeing what I saw that cloudy afternoon in May.

We were rounding up the herd for slaughter, and 5825 was up for jury duty in this batch. We weren't quite friends, but it tugged at me to see a familiar face go. The cattle marched obliviously through the process flow, and thanks to the humane mechanism we used, the cows after them were unaware of what transpired beyond those doors. When the herd had all entered the cattle pushing machine and the gate was closed, my job was finished, so I headed out for a smoke. I stopped dead in my tracks when I heard a bone-chilling scream that will never leave me.

I ran inside and stared in absolute horror, mouth agape, dropping my cigarette to the killing room floor. The stunner never fails to knock them out, but somehow it had. I watched as 5825's now headless body writhed and flailed like a blood-spraying acrobat, kicking off of the hooks of the conveyer and landing on the concrete floor on all four hooves, bellowing that horrendous scream from vocal cords that somehow still functioned.

The floor workers scrambled in terror. Huddling and yelling, they scampered back in their smocks with rubber-gloves and boots, trying to get some distance between them and the unnatural sight.

5825's headless neck bubbled with a spattering of crimson foam, skin sagging slightly to reveal what looked like brain tissue blending out from the red of the muscular neck. Small black marbles were scattered about the exposed, maze-like tissue. The jutting vertebrae was massive, hooked and menacing, like it had grown specifically to be implemented as a razor sharp weapon on this very day. I realized it a mere moment before the carnage ensued, too late to warn them.

5825 reared like a monstrous stallion on two hooves, then charged at the floor workers, heaving his muscular neck in sweeping downward slashes, spraying arcs of red as it split into sanitary capped skulls and severed forearms from elbows. It took only seconds, but three harvest production workers were butchered by the decapitated bull from its bloodied, dagger-like vertebrae emerging from that brain-like meat of the neck. The supervisor, an overweight man named Andy, began to weep then shriek when he realized he was stuck between the bars of a ramp he'd tried squeezing passed. 5828 butchered him with a powerful set of kicks and downward chops. I leaped into a trough in desperation. The thunder of hooves splashed out a good deal of the filthy water I had submerged myself inside of to hide. When I finally emerged, I gasped deeply for air, shivering wet in the foul water.

By the time the police, ambulances and animal control arrived, 5825 was long gone and four people were dead. I told them what occurred; I showed them its severed head. I walked over with them and we observed the gray matter laced with tiny black orbs. We soon realized they were dozens of intermittent, spider-like eyes. Later I learned the skull itself had no brain within aside from the connecting nerves of the eyes, nose and mouth. Scarier still was that vertebrae inside, jagged and knife-like throughout the remains of the upper neck, a mutation clearly meant to be used as a weapon and a tool upon amputation.

I quit the plant the following week. 5825 was never seen again, but I need to get out of this town. The terrifying events took place last year during mating season. Today on my drive to search for jobs, I saw a few young bulls watching my truck as I drove by the fenced field. I stared at the blank disinterested faces of those dark-furred bull calves, marked only on their foreheads with an all too familiar white 'S'.

THE DISTURBING ARCADE GAME IN KABUKICHO

I'd been in Japan a few days visiting my oldest and best friend Brian who'd been living there teaching English. We'd hiked up and down stairs and hills to see Shinto shrines, Buddhist temples, Tokyo Tower and the like and our feet were blistered and ready for a break. He suggested a change of pace by Kabukicho, which I heard was a bit over the top and a tad bit seedy, so of course I obliged. When in Tokyo, right? We hopped on the Shinjuku subway line after the rush hour crush, being stared at as the gaijin (non-Japanese) we were, exited the subway doors and descended upon the neon-lit nightlife.

The sidewalks were flooded with shoppers, tourists, salarymen and costumed characters, as well as a few ladies in revealing clothing, who swiveled our heads before Brian made me laugh by raising his eyebrows and crossing his eyes; the goofball. Everyone tried to pull us into their bars, massage parlors and arcades, but our empty stomachs led us first into a spot for some beers and wagyu beef sushi, which was incredible. A bit later, Brian said he'd noticed a hidden arcade down a street we'd passed, and wanted to check it out since the last remaining once named "Vortex" had shut down a while back.

He led me down some winding streets off the heavily trafficked paths and down a narrow alley with a few dim lights. We approached a slender bouncer in a leather jacket who looked us up and down a few times before waving us in, patting us on our shoulders as we passed.

Once in, we descended carpeted red stairs that led into a corridor of bright screens, dated neon decorations where digital melodies weaved together in chaos. The place was lacking any customers aside from a drunk businessman slumped over their drinks.

The standard game cabinets lined the hall. Fighting games, racing games and pachinko were nothing new, but some oddball Japanese games with strange interfaces caught my eye and begged me to try some obscure games unique to Japan. There was a Korean game "Boong-Ga Boong-Ga" with a strange finger joystick you poke violently into a plastic butt, which was a riot albeit a bit disturbing.

There were a few peculiar spins on dancing games with the foot pads which we tried. I even tried a table flipping game, which was a riot, and then I saw something off to the side that looked like a sculpture from a carousel more than a video game. It was a gloss plastic, life-size knight in front of a screen that wrapped in 180° around the figure. I walked over, entranced, trying to decipher the instructions based on the illustrations printed on the base.

You apparently stepped onto the footprints on the floor of the case, which closes around you, and sensors inside are triggered by you, controlling character movements your confined body was unable to perform. I absolutely had to try this despite being a bit claustrophobic, and fed 200 Yen (about $1.75) into the machine. Blue and orange LED strips lit as the chassis swung open, revealing the area the player stands inside of. It was beyond what I'd seen in the states in terms of VR. The display was clearly visible in the inner screen of the hollow plastic figure that encased me as I stepped inside. I was excited as the armor-like shell closed around me and then inflated around me as air filled rubber tightened snugly on my form. A cooling air filled the vessel as the game began, and I felt a slight elation, pretty sure the game was pumping oxygen into the suit.

The view was phenomenal, a state-of-the-art VR display and incredible sound, depicting a medieval castle interior. 3D rendered goblins wandered around and I quickly got the hang of stiff movement and attacking with the sword to take out the hopping warted enemies.

This was the most immersive game I'd tried. The movement was completely natural despite my body being locked in place. The game itself was nothing too interesting, just attacking a few generic fantasy enemies with pretty realistic animations, but it was impressive nonetheless. I looked forward to taking photos and was trying to figure out how to film the experience for my blog when the first glitch happened.

I had slashed a troll character when static flashed on the screen for a split second and the display changed. The view was grainy video, like a webcam. It showed a room with white porcelain floors and walls, flecked with dark stains. Where the troll had stood, there was a live feed of a figure with vector lines I recognized as tracking sensors around the arms, legs, and head. It was a person, barely recognizable under the layered, tracking software and pixelated video. It took some staring, but it seemed like a woman was underneath the overlaid wireframe visuals, but the video switched back in the game's luscious graphics and I thought it was either glitch or an interesting layered game that had a deeper plot. I continued for a few minutes, but as I came to the next two enemies, brandishing axes and growling with large tusks, the image distorted again and I saw it more clearly.

There were two naked women, bloodied and cowering in the same place the game's enemies were placed. The vector lines seemed to be tracking their real-time movement. I looked in horror through the video display at the metal robotic arm extending into the view screen holding a long, rusty blade instead of the game's shimmering sword I'd controlled. After a second, the feed switched back to the game's visuals, but I no longer felt comfortable playing and tried to leave. I wriggled in place but was stuck in that thick plastic case. I called to Brian, but could tell my voice wouldn't be heard inside of the case and over the digital noise spilling loudly from the other arcade games. I tried to stay away from the enemies, a sense of dread growing, as I was afraid to confront what I knew I was seeing, what I was controlling.

Eventually the case opened, and I walked over and talked to Brian, who seemed concerned but happy to check it out later. I was leaving the next day, so we headed home and just relaxed with some beers and crashed. The next day the flight went seamlessly, and I fell asleep on the plane, all smooth sailing. I was back in the states and ready to return to my normal routine. I prepared a quick lunch when it happened.

I was home, chopping celery for the following day at work, when I had a vivid flashback to the grainy feed. A woman's arm was being chopped up by the robotic arm holding that rusty blade in front of me as blood sprayed outward. I screamed and saw the celery once more, alarmed by the vision as intense and real as when I was in that game. I slept, having nightmares of both the medieval fantasy game and of the poor women being hunted from my point of view. I returned to work the next day, and the hours breezed by.

I'd occasionally have flashes of the naked, screaming women covered in tracking points being stabbed by my robotic arm. It happened when I was running to the bus, picking something up or whenever I was moving quickly. On occasion in those visions, I'd notice well-dressed men with heavy, gold rings on their fingers observing from a higher tier above the killing floor. They appeared to be wealthy observers of the carnage that the robot controlled by the game's player.

In one vision, I saw Brian, naked and bloody, covered with deep wounds on the porcelain floor. I was unable to stop myself from vomiting and after a sparking sound and the smell of burning plastic, everything went black. The chassis opened up and I stood, stunned and shaking, to find myself back in that arcade in Kabukicho, alone and horrified among the melodies and sound effects of the games and lights surrounding me. I called Brian's name, jogging throughout the arcade, but he was nowhere to be found. My phone read 9:45. I'd only been there for about an hour. In my inbox was a message from Brian: *I had a family emergency, emailed you the flight info and a hotel I booked. I will repay you for the taxi, just crash at the hotel tonight please, thank you and talk later.*

I was reeling with horror. I'd been there at the arcade the entire time in a dream state, perhaps induced by flowing fumes in that bizarre arcade game. I staggered on weak legs up the red carpet stairs to the narrow street outside, past the glaring of the bouncer to hail a cab to the modest hotel Brian had reserved. I kept visualizing the cowering women, naked and bloody, who ran in fear from the murderous robot I'd seemed to control through that arcade interface. I began to realize it was just in my head. Maybe I had a small seizure based on the flickering display or most likely just passed out into deep REM sleep from exhaustion from hiking around so much the previous days.

I still haven't spoken to Brian on the phone, but have exchanged texts every so often in the past week since my return, and he seems distant, not his comical self. I almost discounted my fears when seeing his new Instagram pics, but the photos never show him. They are all just different meals these days. Most troublesome was the latest, showing a hand in the corner of the photo of some tasty-looking ramen, but it couldn't have been his hand. It was missing the scar he got from our Flyer sled collision when we were nine. The sense of dread fully emerged as I stared at the hand, on which instead rested a recognizable heavy golden ring next to a little finger missing a tip.

I EXPOSE HAUNTED HOUSE CLAIMS

I work with a small team of ex-professional special effects artists that found a career debunking supposed haunted houses. Perhaps some users of a forum that cherishes ghosts may despise me for it. A lot of good people want to make sure their home is safe, and for peace of mind they call us, so I feel it is our duty to help assure them of their safety when no danger is present. We've found some obvious answers in a number of cases. A gap in the molding causing a room to chill with seeping air, a ticking clock lodged between the walls during the house's renovations, a family of squirrels living within the insulation, etcetera.

Nothing really stood out as possibly supernatural until we got a call from a real estate agent about a woman named Tilly and her uncle's estate.

Tilly was a sweet widow who'd inherited a Gothic mansion from her uncle Jack. The uncle had lived his last years in turmoil over a legal dispute with the real estate agency and had been overly stressed and drinking heavily. He would call Tilly regularly, claiming he'd seen devils everywhere, and dementia seemed a major concern until his demise at the age of 89. After the funeral, Tilly had moved out of her studio apartment and into the mansion, where she explained the house was "severely haunted" and we had to see in person to fully understand.

Excited about what possibly could be in store, but more prepared to find a woman suffering from her inherited dementia, we set out.

This morning we'd arrived, unloading a small set of equipment, microphones, video borescopes to look in small spaces, and plenty of reading material (these jobs tend to be a bit more boring than you'd imagine). I led a team of four usually, but the others had another case, so it was just Norville and I that day. We exited our vehicle and walked up the ancient stairs, signaling our arrival with the heavy, gargoyle-shaped brass knocker. Tilly peaked out from old curtains with wild, watery eyes. She looked absolutely terrified. She opened the door with a finger pressed tightly on her wrinkled, mauve painted lips. She motioned us to come inside, and we did. She whispered, "Thanks for coming, I think it's upstairs now" and almost as if in response, a loud shattering of glass sounded from up the massive, winding staircase.

We walked up the stairs and saw a teacup and saucer shaking on a cabinet, rattling as if it, and only it, was effected from some violent vibration. "Fuck!" my partner shouted, and almost as if triggered by the word, the chinaware cup and saucer propelled itself towards us, smashing above our heads, showering us with porcelain shards. "Get the camera out," I stated. "Film everything," and we slowly walked to the cabinet, which almost immediately burst into flames.

"Fire extinguisher!" I screamed, charging down the stairs with my partner Norville. "Where!?" I asked Tilly, who held her arms tightly, huddled near the wall. She ran into the kitchen and fetched it for me, and I ran up the stairs once more to extinguish the growing flames in a spray of chemical mist. Disaster averted, we searched the charred cabinet, badly burned and now white and wet from the extinguisher contents. There was nothing else out of the ordinary, so we continued to the next room, which housed a large mirror in an ornate wooden frame and a roaring fireplace under high ceilings. The massive, marbled glass mirror looked ancient. Twisting carvings of women in gowns decorated the woodwork framing it. We walked past it and I stared in absolute horror as my reflection transformed.

At first it looked like my face was sagging, but I quickly realized it was melting, blood dripping from my mouth and nose, exploded eyeballs oozing liquid from their sockets. I reached up and my reflection's hands did the same, its face dropping off in chunks to reveal a fleshy skull, charring black from unseen flame. I screamed "KEEP FILMING!" to Norville, who looked absolutely horrified behind the shaking camera. I looked at the fireplace ahead and saw tentacles within.

In that elegant Windsor Court fireplace, gnarled writhing snakes rose from the ground beneath the fire, spewing forth and curling as they grew, yellow chalky and knobbed. It was ungodly, Lovecraftian. They stretched past the mantle into the room as Norville just kept repeating "Jesus Jesus Jesus Jesus," like a skipping record. I had seen this one before however, and I confidently walked to the fireplace, covering my mouth and nose with my left sleeve to pick up the brittle "tentacles", which crumbled in my right hand. "What... what?!" Norville asked, looking on the verge of a full mental breakdown.

"Pharaoh's Serpent," I said boastfully, though the scientists on YouTube should take the credit for solving this particular mystery.

"Mercury Thiocyanate, an exothermic reaction from a volatile chemical. I do believe we're being conned" and I walked over to the mirror, prying along the edge to find it stuck to the wall. "There's a projector behind this, some sort of tracking software hooked up to a rig." I led Norville back over to the bookcase in the other room, to the shattered teacup and dangled it before his camera by the near invisible fishing line tied to the handle. It was almost entirely dissolved by the flames. "I do believe we found our ghost," I stated, eyeing the stairs down.

We approached Tilly, who stood there with a snide look on her face, arms crossed defiantly. She spoke in a bitter tone, "I would have gotten away with it too, if it weren't for you meddling people." I walked over to her and said, "You needed to keep the house but get rid of the real estate problem. Faking your death was the perfect solution, and having a haunted house would kill the attempts to acquire the mansion.

"Didn't it, dear uncle JACK?!" I said as I approached the confused expression of the impostor and began pulling at his neck to remove the convincing silicone mask. I pulled as hard as I could, but it was stuck tight. I grunted, yanking mightily; the mask hot and wet with what must be sweat, as silicone has little ventilation. Finally it gave with a mighty rip, and I stared at the now revealed...

Screaming, muscle-wrapped skull, spilling tendons and veins from the pulsating meat. Blood flowed down her dress, spattering the floor with raining crimson splashes. Her wide, lidless eyes twitched and rolled back in their exposed sockets, and the lipless mouth screamed wide with long, yellow teeth. Chunks of face flopped from her jiggling head as she dropped to her knees and then fell, faceless first, into the accumulating puddle of blood on the hardwood floor. We wiped our prints in awkward silence throughout the mansion and fled out of that cursed house back to the driveway. We started the engine, then burned rubber down the street as poor Norville Rogers shivered and cackled through his final descent into madness, having full conversations with his dog about sandwiches and other foods in the back of the van.

I TRIED A SPICY NOODLE SOUP!

Everyone always tells me I should try new foods, that I'm missing out. I have always been called a basic eater compared to my friends and what floods their Instagram feeds. Chicken nuggets, fries, pasta and I'm happy, I like some vegetables, bell peppers but nothing too spicy usually. Anyway, I'd always heard noodle soup was a great dish, and I like noodles, so when a place opened on my block I figured I might as well give it a go! The place was called "The Savoring Noodles" and it was pretty stripped down to be honest.

They were still clearly in the process of opening. Exposed fluorescent lighting flickered a bit, so the ambiance left something to be desired. I walked in and a middle-aged woman beckoned me forward with a spotted hand. She looked really tired, I could only imagine how many hours she'd put in trying to open the place. The interior was stripped down but fairly large, and I was led into a dim back area past buckets of plaster, dark liquids, dust piles, chipped paint and a spill of some sort. The menu was handwritten, which I thought was kind of cute and rustic. I sat on the black leather of the booth trying to pick between the three options before finally settling on the first, figuring it'd be a safer bet and possibly more frequently ordered, as I had no idea what the ingredients were.

There was a strange smell lingering in the stark back area I couldn't quite place. There was a radio playing music but it was very out of tune, crackling static over what sounded like old big band era tunes. When it started repeating, I realized it was a record that was skipping. I glanced to my side and noticed the tile floor had strange black streaks on it beneath the other booths. A jarring bang brought my attention to the swinging doors, where a large man who looked pale and utterly exhausted stood among strange cuts of hanging meat. He was staring in at me. I made a friendly wave gesture and continued texting my friend until the waitress came back.

She seriously needed some makeup, her skin was so pale it was translucent, and I swear I could see her dark blue veins twitch under the cloudy white skin. I pointed to #1, and she took the menu, placing a small cup of water on my table in complete silence. Soon the large bowl arrived; it looked interesting and smelled a bit pungent, but I never tried any truly exotic flavors, so I'm sure it's just the way these ingredients usually smell. I sipped the warm broth, noticing strange flavors and black oily liquid with the paler broth. It was a tad bitter but savory as well. The white, fuzzy cheese bit things tasted peculiar but interesting, a very cool texture to be honest. The meat was some kind I'm not too familiar with, not quite beef and not quite pork, but succulent and tender nonetheless, chunks of it simmering in the dark, swirling broth.

The black meat was strange, though; something was rather odd about it.

I never had any meat that moved in any way but I swear I could feel the ridged, black meat (steak?) moving, sticky and flexing in my throat as I ate it. I'm sure I was just experiencing new flavors for the first time, but it was a bit strange. I ate the meal after Instagramming it for my friends (who's the basic eater now?) and eventually was ready for the bill. I've been waiting a bit for the waitress. They shut off the lights in the front for some reason, but that's OK, I feel pretty tired and might sneak a nap until she comes back with the check. My stomach is burning a little from the spice too. I'm going to lie on my back in the leather padded booth and try to digest. To new things!

MY ROTTWEILER'S FACE

I'm a professed dog lover. I have been my entire life, growing up with fond memories of our family's golden retriever, Samuel. When I was very young, he made a fluffy amber bed, heated and protective over my tiny self, and when he passed away in my teens, I was absolutely devastated, even more so than losing Grandma. Years passed and when I eventually felt self-sufficient, I realized I was ready to get a dog of my own. I visited the local shelter and, when I saw that Rottweiler puppy's adorable face, I knew I had a new best friend.

Cody was a mess at first, peeing absolutely everywhere, but after I was finally able to potty train him, he was the cutest cuddle monster you could imagine. He'd always be smiling with that adorable face of his, rolling over for belly rubs and giving the sweetest eyes that melted your heart if you ate in front of him. He knew how to work the looks to get treats. His expressions were amazingly clear, as if he'd mastered the art of manipulation with his overly emotive face. When he got into the trash, Cody's shivering, lowered eyes and peaking brows showed true remorse and shame. When playing in the dog park, his squinty smile was all too telling and boastful. That all changed after he collapsed.

Cody was chasing sticks in the park a few weeks ago, happy as ever when fell over mid-dash and lay on that wood-chipped dog park for far too long, making me concerned. I jogged over to his side, inspecting his whimpering, floppy head, and noticed an excessive amount of drool seeping from his toothy maw. He was conscious but refused to get up, and my concern grew, so I made an emergency vet appointment.

We were able to see him that day and the vet said it seemed to be a mild stroke, and my pup was prescribed Furosemide and released that afternoon.

Over the next few days, Cody looked depressed, barely moving or eating. I fed him all of the treats he would actually accept to nibble on, and I gave him endless rubs and tried to comfort him but he seemed devastated. Not a single look aside from a droopy sadness crossed his face. A few nights after, I was watching TV and enjoying some leftover pizza when I heard his collar jingle excitedly, perking my ears.

Cody appeared as a shadow in the doorway from the bedroom, panting and staring at me, his white eyes reflecting light in a slightly eerie way. "Come on buddy!", I called so I could see him in the light and not merely a set of creepy glowing eyes. Cody walked a few feet forward into the light and stood there, breathing heavily with a contorted expression on his face that chilled my blood and nearly stopped my heart.

I'd half expected to see that adorable begging face he used to make for pizza. He actually was making a very expressive face despite the stroke, but it was beyond hideous. His right eye was wide and bulging while the left a twisted sliver, his lip curled like in a sneer, fangs showing too much gum, drool glazing his black lips. His shiny nose was twitching, like he was trying with all of his effort to make another face but completely forgot how, almost as though his nerves were connected wrong or if his facial musculature was misplaced entirely. I wanted to make him feel good, so I called him over and fed him pizza and called him a good boy, followed with some pets and reassurance. In retrospect, I wish I hadn't.

I feel now I need to clarify that Cody looked fine when relaxed.

Aside from looking a bit glum, he appeared only mildly droopy on his left side, nothing very noticeable. It was only now that he must have gotten the confidence to return to making what were once adorable sweet faces, but were now chilling, grotesque expressions. He looked insane, deformed and had severely frightened me on a few occasions as I'd turn to see those bulging eyes, twisted nose and quivering fangs in his lopsided mouth, a rippling tongue flicking in the air. There was no way to get used to it despite how hard I tried.

I kept showing him love and affection, aware of his well-being at all times, but he really started to freak me out. I thought some social reintegration might help, so I took him to the dog park. Other dogs at the park refused to face him, they'd whimper and run away to their fearful owners when he'd try to play, and I think that was what made him realize he wasn't conveying his intentions properly. It might have been what pushed him even further, and I, now too, wish I hadn't taken him there. But how could I have ever known?

He began watching TV with me, but usually on the floor by the side of the couch, out of my view. I now recall what I was seeing when I'd looked over to make sure he was there, in between my petting him, his head bobbing seemingly in sync with the dialogue on the TV. I was in my room after one such evening when I woke up from a nightmare to see Cody standing on his hind legs as a kangaroo might at the foot of my bed, *talking*. He was howling out what sounded like fragmented words, those white dots of eyes staring into mine as he seemed to try and mimic human speech in a horrible, warbling manner.

"Urt. Ork. BAD. Kull," Cody said.

"Come here, boy," I called, turning on my nightstand light to reveal that shaking, spitting, bipedal version of my beloved Cody. I watched the bulging eye and quivering jaw as he blurt out a response: "NoooOOoo, ka-koOOo," Cody then seemed finally able to say it, "COMMMMME," trailing in a deep, gurgling growl. He stood there seething, face contorted into what appeared a nightmarish grin, ropes of saliva webbing his jaws to the floor below his two planted feet. He seemed defiant, not like he was trying to communicate with or impress me, more like he was trying to be the one giving orders, Orwellian as it may sound. I slept with the door locked that night, beyond nervous as I slowly guided the growling Cody out of my room. That night the door knob rattled me awake a few times, followed by that word I wish I'd misheard. "Meaat." I scheduled a vet visit for the following day.

That afternoon I'd convinced Cody to follow me into the car, but not with treats like before, however. I had needed to use that night's dinner, a raw NY strip steak to coax him, slivers at a time. Upon arriving, the vet's concern was instant. He nearly yelped in shock at his appearance, and he insisted on a CAT scan, (or DOG scan as the vet called it). He tried to laugh, but the trembling in his voice betrayed fear thicker than blood. He was almost shivering, absolutely horrified when he finally explained he had some results.

The vet told me Cody's CAT scan revealed an abnormal brain tumor, and that he apparently hadn't had a stroke. They ran a blood test and Cody's blood type had switched from the common DEA 6 to something like DEA 11, something he explained is completely impossible based on everything he knew from veterinary school. He said the tumor appeared to have a cerebellum as well as a cortex. It was strikingly similar to the growing brain of a small child. He then asked things that scared me.

He'd asked me if I'd experimented on Cody, if I'd ever cut him, if I was sure it was my dog. He asked about Cody's siblings, where the shelter was where I'd gotten him, about contamination or chemical contact, of any possible radiation exposure. His questions began to make me far more concerned, the opposite of my hopes. The vet was terrifying me. When we returned to the room where Cody had been lying in, sedated, he was gone.

It had been two days since I'd seen that nightmarish, twisted face of my dog, or what possibly was once my dog. I almost felt a relief as ashamed as I am to admit it. That way he stood on two legs, defying me. The way he'd twisted my doorknob and spoke the word "meat" was beyond unsettling. I wondered if he ran away to evolve into something else somehow or if he had a parasitic twin in his canine brain that was somehow taking control, or if it was some mutation making him smarter albeit far more sinister.

Last night as I took out the trash, I heard that horrible voice that shouldn't be. "Come. M.M..Meat," the voice said from the shadows, two white circles reflecting the cold moon from the fence near my neighbor's yard. What once was Cody turned his furry black head to their house, and I saw the horrific, gnarled expression of my Rottweiler's face before he vanished behind the fence. It wasn't until today, as I watched in horror as the ambulances showed up to my neighbor's and took away Mrs. Daulton's body, that I'd realized what he'd done.

I FOUND JERRY TODAY

I'm no saint, but I do occasional volunteer work in Manhattan on the weekends. Once a month, I head to a midtown church and shovel mac and cheese and turkey meals to a grateful, disheveled lot who have been discarded by society. Sure, some are drunks, some addicts, but they are all people, mostly good people, and as fall steals the warmth from the air and brings chill to the night, I make sure I remember how hard the coming months will be for them.

At my shelter, there's often an older gentleman, perhaps in his 70s, Jerry, who had been a rising stand-up comic in his heyday before his one liner style lost its mass appeal. On rare occasions, he'd entertain us with a few old-fashioned yet funny dad jokes. Jerry was hilarious in his own way, and everybody loved watching him deliver his wholesome yet adorably antique brand of humor.

He was almost always around, sharing stories with a chuckle about Vegas, Hollywood, dinners with George Burns and other wild yet true tales. The cocaine trend of the late 70s and a series of very poor choices with finances and females left him bankrupt in the 90s and homeless since the mid 2000s. He had a ton of charisma and many friends, so when he went missing two weeks ago, all of us at the soup kitchen became concerned. We made a pact to take some time to look around to make sure he was OK, hoping he'd found a place to move into and stumbled upon better luck. I encountered him first a few nights ago when I saw the figure in the stairwell.

It was fully night, and I'd finished picking up a few photos I'd had printed, dashing through a dwindling mess of people exiting some concert that spilled onto the sidewalk with a flood of tobacco and drunk conversation. I meandered into the street to escape the mob and saw a familiar face swaddled in a few large blankets in the shadow of an old basement club's stairwell. It was a recently closed nightclub, likely the rent doubled, and was abandoned until another sucker was willing to pay the bloated monthly fee, a perfect place to camp out undisturbed for Jerry. I approached, noticing he looked a bit thin in the shadows and grew concerned.

"Jerry! Good to see you, buddy. We all miss you over at the church. How've you been?" I asked with genuine concern and a bit of relief.

"Doin' fine, can't complain!" he said in a surprisingly chipper voice. "Been making good money in this area so I haven't needed the church food, but I'll stop back real soon," he said, and a wave of warm relief washed over me.

"That's wonderful to hear, Jerry. You have my cell, just let me know if you ever need anything," I said, glad he was doing OK. I peeked a look in the hat in front of him, noticing a bunch of fives, tens, and even a few twenties. He was apparently doing very well for himself here with the drunken concert goers. "So how's the grind?" I asked a bit out of curiosity at this point. He seemingly had over $200 in that small hat.

"The show goes on, the derelict dummy act is a hit!" he said, bringing a smile to my face. I got a kick from the idea of him ranting in cathartic one liners about the trials and tribulations of homelessness.

"I hope I can see it soon!" I said, placing a blueberry muffin near his gloved hand. I said my goodbyes, glad that all was well, and continued home on the subway with my photo prints.

A few days passed as I'd been kept busy by my day job and my photography on the side. Today I finally had some extra time waiting for prints, so I figured I'd bring a snack to Jerry in case he needed it. I approached the venue's empty sidewalk, glad to avoid a mob, and proceeded to the stairwell, noticing a few people gathered in front of it.

Perfect opportunity, I thought. I wanted to see the new routine, so I leaned over until I was able to get a view. Jerry was telling entirely new jokes, hilarious but extremely vulgar and self-deprecating. The well-dressed men watching were in absolute stitches by the act. They clearly had plenty of money and were spilling it into his cup freely, which at least made me a bit happy.

When they finally cleared, He'd made a few hundred easy, and I approached, applauding. "That was insanely hilarious, Jerry!" I said with a grin, and I wasn't exaggerating. He had a serious knack for obscene humor I hadn't previously known. "Seems like you're earning more than me now, you can get your own place soon I bet!"

He was laying in the same position as last time, and something about that unnerved me a bit. I have a good eye for detail, so when I noticed the folds of the blankets and placement of that hat in the exact same place, I grew concerned. Even that muffin I'd brought a few days ago was near his hand, unwrapped. I asked if he'd been here the past few days and approached but he raised a hand and spoke.

"I found my lane, stay in yours, buddy! I drive a shopping cart full of trash and piss myself so you may want to stay a few lanes over too!" he spat out jokingly, and I feigned laughter but was a little grossed out and concerned about his self-insulting comedy. I also had noticed something was wrong with his manner of speaking. It was the way his jaw moved. It somehow seemed unnatural, his Adam's apple hadn't appeared to be moving.

"Jerry?" I asked with a building shiver in my neck as I looked at him closer, smelling the decay. He was beyond pale, his eyes looked puffy and red as I inched closer. I then saw the slight glimmer of eyes in the darkness of the folded blanket behind him.

"I'd stay back if I was you. In the rare times I get mouthwash, it's to drink it!" Jerry said, and then I saw them. I saw the long white teeth under disturbed, wild eyes, moving as whoever was behind Jerry's body in the shadows caused him to appear to speak. I stumbled back, realizing what I was seeing in a flood of absolute horror, and I ran.

The paramedics and police arrived not long after I called. I walked back only after I'd seen them and felt safe enough to return. I spoke with them, answered dozens of questions about Jerry, and confirmed my darkest thought as to what had transpired. Whoever was in the blankets with Jerry's corpse was gone by then, the money and hat as well. Jerry had been deceased over a week, and somewhere, whoever had puppeted his corpse was hiding in the shadows, watching.

THE ABORTION

My mother, my sister and I grew up in a rural home with a lawn and nearby woods. We had a chipper Scottish Terrier, Herbert, who ran about smelling flowers and deer droppings and wagging his black nubby tail. Childhood was lovely and my mother was fairly open about most things, such as our father running off when I was young, a hopeless alcoholic. When my sister and I grew of age, we were advised about flying things like birds, bees and the likes, and it was then we learned of the abortion.

My mother was very religious growing up. She was lovely and kind but extraordinarily strict about things that conflicted with her beliefs. She'd explained that the child, who'd she named Roger, had chromosomal abnormalities that caused him to stop developing in the womb. To her dismay, the doctors had advised her to abort out of health concerns. She had reluctantly gone to the clinic alone as my father had been out on a 3 day bender. I gather she explained this as a warning about irresponsible sex, and that was the only time she mentioned it.

Years passed and I grew older, went on dates, started college, and wiped away heartbroken tears. I'd recently been depressed and everything in the city reminded me of my ex, so I made plans this weekend to spend time with my mom back home. I texted about four hours ago that I'd be home around 2, and I received no response. I bought my ticket and a paperback novel to accompany the three-hour train ride. I dozed off, arrived at the station and called my mom, getting her voicemail. I called a car and soon entered the slick black vehicle, careening past spindly branches of autumn trees and country sky. Mom was often in her study, away from her phone, so concern hadn't yet built.

We pulled into the driveway, and I thanked the driver who drove off to his next fare. I inhaled the fresh country air and childhood flooded back as I headed down the walkway to the unlocked front door.

"Mom? I'm home!" I called into the house, to no response. Talk radio filled the kitchen, a half chopped onion sat on the cutting board, wrinkled and clearly days old. Panic flooded my mind in the realization something might have happened. "MOM!" I called loudly, frantically running up the stairs. Nothing, there was no sign of her anywhere. After searching the entire house, I realized she was gone and decided to call my father, and that's when the dread grew inside of me.

He picked up after the fourth ring, and I explained I came home and she wasn't there. I asked if he'd heard from her, and if I could see him, as I was a bit worried. I told him about the onion, half cut on the counter, and I heard his tone change from friendly to grave. "Oh.. oh god.." he said, sounding like he knew something I didn't, something dreadful. "Don't go in the basement, I'm driving over right now," he said in a panicked voice.

"Uh, dad, we don't have a basement," I stated, as if he'd forgot that in the fifteen years he'd been gone. There was an attic, a porch, a walkway, a garage and 2 bathrooms, all of which I'd checked thoroughly in search of my mom, but there was no basement. He then began to talk about his drinking while I scanned the floors in each room, walking over to my mother's study.

"I started drinking after leaving your mother," he said to the sound of an engine starting, a shiver in his voice, "Not before. I started drinking when I realized what she had done." I noticed the open closet door in her study that was always closed, my phone pressed firmly to my ear. "You were only three at the time, I didn't mean to abandon you, but I couldn't stay there, knowing." He began crying, completely bawling, and I saw the tiny knob on the closet wall, the seams near the edges of the barely visible self-closing door.

I opened the door to stairs that descended in darkness into the basement. My feet led me in despite the fear that raised my neck hairs and thumped in my chest. My father continued, "She said she went to the clinic that day but she lied," he sobbed. The basement was cold and pitch black, so I touched the button to reactivate my phone screen, which was pressed firmly against my ear. "She never had the abortion," he whimpered. The white glow was too faint. I heard the rustling sound and removed my father's sobbing from my ear to illuminate the shadows in front of me and I saw what had been making the sound.

It was about five feet tall, its smooth, slightly translucent head massive and malformed. It was white and puffy, dark veins visible under soft, gelatinous skin. Its black billiard ball eyes reflected the phone screen, unfeeling as it stared at me, over the half-eaten corpse of my mother. It was my brother Roger, somehow kept alive in tanks that lined the walls until he grew into that thing. He was a standing fetus with a few developed adult parts, his thin fingers, his crooked teeth, his bony feet. His brain was slightly visible in the massive forehead above those voids of eyes. Above that horrible toothy mouth that, as I screamed while scrambling up the stairs in absolute terror, screamed back at me.

MY PLASTIC SURGERY WAS A SUCCESS

My physician advised me against it, my friends expressed consistent disapproval and my family treated me like a stranger after I begged them to help finance plastic surgery. Everybody said I looked fine, "completely normal", attractive even and the like, as they always do.

They smile at you and they lie, secretly trying to boost their egos by having a freak standing next to them, the stars of their group photos. It is only when doors open in the form of inspiration you realize there is absolutely no reason to keep playing their pitiless, selfish games. When you have to look in the mirror, day in and day out, staring at that bulbous nose, those gigantic nostrils, those tiny, beady eyes and bulky jaw, those doors open to reveal a solution.

People don't realize how sensitive the trigeminal nerve is, looping and branching out in forking paths that spread throughout the face. You'd think a simple shot of the lidocaine you pocketed from the last defiant doctor visit would quell it, but you'd be very wrong. You may think the Tylenol-Codeine NO.3 you owned would fuzz out that intense, screaming pain, but you'd be wrong yet again. Once that steak knife punctures the skin and cuts along the ridge of your jawbone, the pain permeates you. It grabs you by your dripping skull and screams directly into your wide, tear-filled eyes.

You might think jaw muscles are like rare steak, that you can gently saw the blade back and forth and sliver away, carving neat little slices from the edge; like I thought. If so, you'll be surprised when they flex, seeming to hug the blade when tensing, trying to halt their own atrophy in a fit of resistance. Dozens of fibrous strands all trying in vain to prevent their own demise, the ugly, bulging muscles that made you a freak unwilling to leave on decent terms. All of the face muscles become a hideous, stubborn resistance, and you need to dig hard and deep, forcing that blade until the pain screams, until they scream. Blood gushes out, hot and slick until it dries, coagulating into an iron-rich crust. The muscles are brazen and stubborn, but the bone offers its own trials as well.

The vibrations as you hammer the screwdriver into your skull are intense, to say the least. If you've had dental work involving a drill, you may understand the concept, but a heavy blow from an effective chisel will propel that feeling to a new level. Flashes of white blind you with each strike, and a scraping sound you both hear and feel is hard to conceive until you begin. As blood lubricates your skull, the screwdriver slips, and aiming precise and true at those malformed defects you can only blame genetics for becomes increasingly difficult.

The chipped pieces spill out onto the newspaper you placed in front of the mirror, flecked with blood, defiant to the end, but even that feeling is nothing compared to the filing.

Cheese graters are in every kitchen, but aged gouda wills itself apart generously compared to the rigid and enduring mountains of a deformed human skull. After a few failed efforts, the file from the garage seemed the only viable option. That vibration unfocuses the eyes as you file away the ugly, bulky zygomatic bone that god cursed you with. The pieces fleck your red, sticky hands like powdered sugar as progress is made, as your true shape is revealed underneath. The pesky, bulging nose proves to be the real fighter, however, but it too will succumb to beautification.

That ugly ridge that haunted you your entire life will prove to be the final bout, jutting out in utter defiance. Once the skin is split and peeled aside, both cartilage and bone stand inter-locked in spite, oozing red. The file seemed smart at first, but a revelation may give insight into a different combination of tools. You might discover that a hammer and a knife perform twice the work in half the time, and you will be rewarded for that discovery. The hammered blade clears most of that hide-ous ridge of nose cartilage before locking into the nasal bone, stuck in place like a stubborn mule. This is the triumphant last battle, and it will be one for the ages. You hammer upward onto the blade with the rings and crunches, hearing, feeling, the cracks that slowly build with each jarring slam. You contemplate giving up as your eyes are filled with blood and tears, but you must persist. Just as you might expect to topple from blood-loss, it snaps, creating a clean runway of a beautiful, perfectly straight nose.

A quick shower blooms red, and seems to never stop turning the water pink, but eventually, once it's done, you already can see in that mirror just how beautiful you now look. You smile, although it's hard to really identify the expression after the work on your previously deformed lips, and you exhale deeply, knowing you are finally fixed.

Everything throbs, leaking even after three rolls of absorbent paper towels had sopped up unending springs of red. But you are a vision of perfection, and you walk outside to shine as you've always deserved.

People are clearly unable to perceive the immaculate perfection before them. They are overwhelmed, aroused, enticed, covering their mouths with the inability to suppress their emotion at the magnitude of the work. People bellow out in a guttural response of unabashed envy, tears welling in their eyes. Riders on the bus photograph it so to never forget the day they witnessed beauty in its purest form. People realize how hideous they are in comparison to me now and they scream in fury, in jealous rage at their inadequacy and it's clear to see; my plastic surgery was a success.

STAYED OUT THERE TO BE ALONE

I've had terrible luck with women. Truth be told, I am likely the problem and don't shy away from admitting it. I had a horrific breakup that left me the chaff of a broken man with my ego destroyed. I just wanted to get away from every cynical smile and backstabbing, cheating friend. I wanted to be alone in nature, among the deer and the trees, away from the traffic and the selfish gluttons that sat in it. I had watched the documentary "Alone in the Wilderness", the story of Richard Proenneke and felt this was my destiny as I lay on the floor in a pool of tears and whiskey. I sold it all and headed to Utah with a backpack, a hooptie and a dream.

I learned fast how repetition in any manner can drive you insane. The increasingly tasteless oatmeal I boiled daily became a chore to force down. The thin bedding in my tent felt more like paper over rock each night. The endless woods transformed from beautiful and serene to melancholy and dreary. The quiet, however, was astounding, and all of the qualms and bickering in my head were drowned in a pool of bliss by the soothing insects, the breeze, and the lapping water flowing through the river. The birds woke me early each morning, but I forgave them, and so I became accustomed to my new wall-less home in the woods.

Supplies ran thin soon, and I learned quickly how to aim the bow I'd purchased along with dozens of arrows. I had flint, but refillable lighters and butane canisters were more effective to start a cooking fire. Rabbit was my usual meal, they bred as advertised so there seemed to be no shortage up here. I'd fish every other day, trout and bass were always on the menu, but they stopped showing up a few nights ago altogether. So did the rabbits, and as if that wasn't worry enough, so did the morning birds, replaced with the whistling wind and near silence. It was as if something drove them all away.

There was no explanation, and I'd assume they'd return, but after a few days in absolute solitude with not a visible living being, my hunger grew and I decided to take a trip into town for supplies. I tried to start the engine, but the clicking sound taunted me like a snickering menace from within the chassis. I had a good battery, so it was unfortunately the starter. Why did I have to buy the cheapest damn car? I cursed myself, a creeping fear tickling my mind.

I spent the day hunting down edible plants, mainly clover and chickweed, not quite enough fuel for the 13 hour walk to Mountain View, but enough to hit a main road and hitch a ride into the nearest town. My stomach was growling and the dead of the woods began to magnify in a peculiar way. The howling of the wind, at first a blowing breeze, began to sound more like a sucking in, a forceful breathing, and I stopped dead in my tracks as I realized it wasn't just the wind alone.

Something was making a similar sound, and I spun to face the source.

There was a slim figure, tall but hunched, breathing in heavy, long wheezes, staring at me from perhaps twenty meters back. It was completely nude and severely deformed; the face appeared almost split down the center from a vertical gash that resembled a horrific folding inward. Jutting ribs and lanky arms made it no less haunting as it watched me from behind the lattice of trees. It had no hair, just smooth scalp and a haunting face that was terrifying from even this distance. I quickened my pace, checking my compass to make sure I was heading northeast every so often. The sucking breath sounds only increased, and soon I looked back to see the figure was only a dozen meters away.

It was maybe six feet tall, eyes inset in lumped, malformed sockets over the cleft face that shocked me outright. It looked almost like a blade wound that had healed improperly due to its extreme severity. Their hands looked stained red with blood, holding something that looked like a human organ. I took the bow from my shoulder and pointed it at the figure shouting "Stay back!" but it kept hobbling over moss and twigs in my direction, breathing that unnatural, creepy wheezing sound. Terror overtook me. I was in the middle of a vast wilderness with whoever or whatever this was, homing in on me. I began to run as absolute fear pierced my psyche.

My heart beat rapidly and my head filled with thoughts of how long I'd be out there before my body was found, if there would even be a body left to find. The sun was setting, and I'd need to stop to get my flashlight, which meant I would lose precious ground to my pursuer. To make matters worse, the compass read west; I must have messed up rounding the last ravine. My feet in my boots were wet and cold, and my legs were growing tired. I swiveled my backpack to my front mid-run to fetch the light but dropped my lighter to the ground with a butane bottle from the motion. I realized I had to leave them. With the flashlight now in my hand, I'd be able to see the compass clearly as well as the trails that lay ahead. But I didn't see the cliff edge in time. A rock met my face in a hideous collision when I fell a few meters down.

I came to in the dead of night. No crickets, no insects, just that horrible wheezing sound coming from above. I was completely trapped, looking up at my pursuer, whose shiny, malformed head was a back-lit from the moon as it stared down at me, breathing those fluid-filled, sucking breaths. My stomach screamed and my ankle felt like it had been rolled, and I knew there was no escape. My arrows were nowhere to be felt nor my flashlight, so I lay still as possible, trying to play dead as a last resort. Something heavy and slimy landed on my chest with a slap, and I eventually passed out.

I awoke to find the corpse of a skinned rabbit on my chest, as well as the lighter and butane I'd dropped in panic. I immediately started a fire and cooked the gifted food to sate my aching belly. I saw no sign of that figure, and I eventually limped my way to a road, and in less than an hour, a driver slowed to pick me up and offered to drive me to town. Benny, or "Binne", as he introduced himself, was fascinated by my story. He'd explained a private plane crashed somewhere in those woods a few months earlier. The pilot's family was found dead, but his body never turned up, assumed to have been eaten by bears. Then Benny and I both understood. Seriously deformed from the plane crash and fire after having lost his family, he likely had stayed out there to be alone as well.

THERE WAS A JUMP CUT IN THE NEWS

I have an obsession with nitpicking details in films and television. I can't control it or ignore it and it's so ingrained in me as to fully spoil all attempts to be a passive viewer. I see when an actor jumps three feet to the left in a cut shot, a hand switches to a different position breaking the fluidity, an item vanishes etcetera and it drives me crazy each and every time. As I watched the news a few nights ago, I saw a continuity error that made absolutely no sense, and that's how this whole nightmare began.

It was the local cheesy daily news as usual, a vague and neutral delve to politics and some local crime stories to keep you consuming and afraid, a fluff story about a child's last wish to donate all their charity money to rescuing puppies, yadda yadda yadda. The final "fuck off" salute to end the broadcast is what caught my eye when it came earlier than expected. The reporter shuffled papers that then simply vanished. It was subtle. I knew something was off at first without realizing exactly what. They were gone off the table altogether, and I knew immediately, this was a poorly seamed together jump cut. Something had been removed. The clock read 10:22 to confirm it was eight minutes short; a segment had been completely cut out.

DVR is my copilot, and I rewound and played that final segment back dozens of times. I saw the wide-eyed stare caught in the last frame before the cut. I saw the terror on the newscaster's face in that one sloppily edited frame. I saw the subtle difference in the hair, in the way the blazer hung misaligned on his shoulders, it didn't match at all. As I scrubbed back and forth, I finally noticed the reflection in his shiny black mug of likely spiked coffee; a reflection of something white getting larger, getting closer to him before the cut.

I have an obsession; I scour the IMDB profiles of nearly everyone I watch. You can call me a stalker, a geek, a freak, I don't care. It's my obsession that helped me dig through names, numbers and addresses, to track the locally residing newscaster in his large suburban abode. I was able to find his number from a simple deduction in the yellow pages, and when I called, it went straight to voicemail. The next day I decided to find out what had happened, and drove to his fenced in, custom built, brick and stone home. His wife was on the phone, tears sweeping down trails of eyeliner; she was visibly distraught. Her husband, the newscaster, clearly wasn't home, so last night I did what any obsessed person is liable to do: I drove to the station. There was no way to expect what I found, no matter how attentive to detail I'd been.

The station building was in the heart of the city, so it was nearly forty minutes of nighttime driving. I parked in the garage and immediately recognized his car. I have an extremely obsessive personality, so I knew it was his. That shiny S-class Mercedes he'd slipped a quip in about years back when referencing a Bond movie, shimmering in the fluorescent flicker was unmistakable; he'd never left the building. I walked to the elevator, pressing the number I'd researched earlier and soon reached his floor, to pale overhead lights in an empty hallway, leading to the slightly ajar glass door to the network's studio.

The smell of death is unmistakable, a choking stench that painfully enters your lungs, forcing you to cough at the noxious bodily gasses. The smell was unbearable as I entered, and I needed to remove my jacket and press it hard against my nose to filter out the horrible odor. I saw multiple bodies, decaying and beyond facial recognition, screaming teeth and bruising skin rotting off the skulls and the hands.

There were dozens of bodies. I recognized a few by their clothing; some newscasters, some reporters, the weatherman, an oozing and maggot filled face under that unmistakably perfect television hair. Only one light was on, and I followed it stealthily back to the editing room.

The man at the computer looked almost skeletal from starvation, but alive. He'd been malnourished and emaciated to the point his body had been eating its protein. The hollow of his cheeks sunk inward below wild, wide eyes that twitched in pure terror as he worked deep into the night. His tears streamed and snot dripped down to a horrible grimace.

He appeared to have been working nonstop for days due to his thick, purple eyelids; swollen and wet. The scrubbed timeline in his edit played audio back as he perfectly patched together soundbites, apparently to create tomorrow's news content, covering the day's events. I then noticed the thin, bony white hand with too few fingers reach to the back of his head, and finally saw it.

It was a slim figure with soggy white skin that hung on the frame like wet paper towels on silverware. The face was hideous, far too much of its black gums were exposed in that sagging, wide mouth under those hollow looking pits of eyes. Its tiny nubs of teeth jutted outward from the black chasm of a mouth at a harsh angle. It was almost human, but so clearly not.

I watched as its arm slowly extended to the back of the editor's head, removing small chunks of red flesh from the skull, before retracting the arm and feeding the bits into its ghastly black mouth. I stared in horror, then noticing the screen behind that thing, realizing why the news broadcast jumped when it had. The story segment removed was frozen on a flat screen monitor at the editing table. It was a freeze frame of that field reporter, whose decayed body now lay oozing out on the newsroom floor, standing on the roof under a disk in the sky.

I WOKE UP LIKE THIS

I woke up to the throbbing headache of a hangover of unbelievable proportions. I was wheezing, then began coughing in a fit that went on for far too long. Each cough stung my ribs in an intense sharp pain that signaled fracture. My eyes were sealed to the point I had to physically pry them open. Every part of me ached. I looked down at my bloody hands, the deep gouges in my arms and the red stains on my sheets and I began to panic. There were massive lacerations all over my arms and legs, which were flecked with dried blood and clearly in need of stitches. I tried to remember how drunk me ended up like this and the image flashed in my head.

I was horribly drunk last night, blackout drunk. I remember getting cut off at the bar and staggering home, but something had clearly happened on the way. I remember a face; it was pale, and the teeth were far too long. Something was off about it, but I couldn't remember who or what or where. I rose out of the blood-stained mess of my bedding and limped over to the bathroom to relieve myself. I then eased my butchered body into the tub as carefully as possible, washing off so many layers of blood that they never seemed to stop the water from turning red.

I sat in the warm tub until it cooled to room temperature, then carefully lifted my battered frame from the draining pink water. I limped over to my room to put on my least favorite and expendable underwear, socks, pants, and shirt. My face was swollen and bruised purple and I felt like I'd been hit by a train. I picked up my newly cracked phone screen and saw the dozens of texts and emails.

Jeff (my good friend): "Are you alright?!?!"
Mom: "Call us now! We're worried!!!"
Dan (another friend): "Holy shit I just saw the video"
Unknown: "Thank you so much… I can never repay you"
Matt: "What the fuck was that thing????!!!"
Unknown: "Ay, it's Juan man, I filmed that whole thing, got your number from your friend."

One of my friends had linked to a popular media blog where people post fight videos frequently, and the link showed a figure that was clearly me, my face blushed deep red. 132,043 views. Ugh, dear Jesus, what the hell did I do? I clicked play, held my breath and watched.

In the video, a woman was bloody and screaming on the ground in an alley and in front of her was what looked like a naked man but unnaturally tall and with something horribly wrong with his mouth. It had long, thin teeth that were not at all human, and his eyes were red as billiard balls, jutting out far too much from the pale, wrinkled face.

"Holy fuck!" the cameraman said before shouting out for help. The woman screamed and suddenly, my staggering figure entered the frame, spilling out a flood of trash talk.

I was insulting that thing and antagonizing it away from the girl in the video, who was able to escape once the attention turned to me. I watched the video play as my drunken self slurred, "That's all I can stands and I can't stands no more." I wound up a punch like a Popeye cartoon, and actually landed the comical, drunken blow on the freakish figure's elongated jaw with a dull pop. Clearly infuriated, it fell to all fours like a strange insect, then charged at me, slashing me in the thigh with black, talon-like nails.

The cameraman said, "Holy shit, this drunk dude's fighting this crazy freak," and kept filming as I sloppily mimicked Ali's dancing footwork. I kept slurring quotes from pop culture, Street Fighter 2 and 80s movies lines like "tiger uppercut," "I came here to kick ass and chew bubblegum," and the like, bleeding from each vicious attack from that thing, slashing my legs, knocking me to the ground as it flayed off chunks of my forearm. Shocking amount of blood sprayed out, but somehow the booze had kept me afloat and had subdued the pain. I watched as I eventually slammed that thing's head into a wall, leaving it stunned.

I'd pounded the attacker, kicking its skull saying "I'm Ronaldo, bitch!" and other drooled quips that struck a chord as hilarious despite the horrific wounds I'd sustained, spilling ribbons of hanging skin from each of its attacks. Eventually, it scuttled on all fours into a manhole, which it lifted with seemingly no effort and it slithered within as I sang out "No, I don't want no C.H.U.D.s!" before vomiting a truly disgusting amount on the ground to the accompaniment of a cheer and laughter from the few witnesses. The girl in the video thanked me and the guys made some more remarks, asking what the hell that thing was before the video cut. I sat there completely in shock. I guess drunk me gets a medal for handling whatever that thing was that came out from underground last night. Sober me is heading to the hospital.

THE WALK TO TOMMY'S

Tommy and I left school together as per my mother's advice. She was stuck at the ER; the buses weren't running due to the snowstorm, and I lived much too far to safely get back home. Tommy, on the other hand, lived a mere 10 minutes from our school and as we were good friends, it seemed smartest to go with him until she was able to get me. I liked Tommy enough and looked forward to checking out the epic video game collection he frequently bragged about, so this was perfectly fine with me. My mom explained she talked to his mother previously and Tommy was waiting near the entrance, where I found him in his puffy coat, scarf-wrapped ready and gloves locked and loaded like mine, waving.

Flurries filled the sky, dimming the sun to an almost misty veil, beautiful and serene despite the howling wind. The lack of road traffic added to the surreal environment, and I realized how alone we truly were as we started off on the short walk behind the field to Tommy's place. It was too windy to talk. I'd tried a few times, but he cocked his head and squinted, clearly unable to hear amid the heavy gusts, so I figured I'd wait to tell him about the new comic I'd found. A muffled crackling sound seemed to echo from the woods to the right. We both stopped dead, only our wide, uncovered eyes capable of displaying the fear we both felt. "Let's get the hell out of here!" I yelled over the wind to Tommy, who answered by rapidly nodding, and we began trudging as fast as the snow would allow.

A sudden gust of wind blinded us when we walked directly into it, freezing my lashes and causing me to squint heavily. "Jesus," I called over, expecting a reply, but only the howling wind was heard as it screamed into my face with an arctic gust and another cracking sound.

"Tommy," I called out, shielding my eyes with my heavy gloves, but I couldn't see him anywhere. I backtracked to see if he'd fallen due to increasingly limited visibility. I then saw his deep footprints a bit back, angling off to my left. After realizing I must have missed him turning, I began to backtrack, following his steps, deep set into the fresh snow while calling out his name to no reply.

A few meters in, the footprints spread as if he was running, and concern grew in my subconscious that quickly changed to fear. The steps seemed not only spaced farther apart as in a sprint, but the left and right prints began to get increasingly farther apart as well, as if his stance had widened exponentially. I realized he might be running side to side in silly steps, playing games, so I said, "Stop goofing around, Tommy, slow the hell down!" trying to not seem like the kid I was. The steps grew impossibly wider apart, three, four, five, six feet between, and they kept increasing until a spattering of red began to fleck the snow in the spaces between them. I began hyperventilating and pulled my inhaler from my pocket when I heard it again.

The horrible cracking shook the forest with an echo, the sound we'd heard before, but this time it sounded less like tree branches and more wet and crisp. I heard what sounded like heavy breathing, barely audible during the breaks from the heavy gusts of wind coming from the trees ahead. On either side of the growing, dark red trail, the footsteps vanished into the heavy woods, where I saw two small reflected circles, the size of human eyes but five feet apart, blink from the shadows within.

I turned back and I ran, following my footprints as best I could with my lungs and heart pounding under my heavy coat. When I got back to the school, Tommy was standing there in his coat, scarf and gloves, asking me where the hell I'd been and why I was shaking so hard. He then led me in the other direction, on that short walk to his house, away from those woods.

THE YAWN

It's strange to think something that signals boredom could be the cause of such nightmarish anguish and misery. People always fear zombies, serial killers, terrorists, active shooters and nuclear attacks as presented by TV and motion pictures. The irony of the events that unravel the world is just another finger in the gunshot wound, twisting painfully as if to shame it. Not a bang, not a whimper. The world ends with a yawn.

I had applied for and been granted my masters to please my parents, not yet enticed by a world of thesis papers and internships. I had ambitions and dreams that soared broader and higher; I'd always felt I was special. I'd not yet been dashed onto the windshield of life as so many are when they seem to realize we are all one and the same.

Quietly with a raised brow, I said, "This guy knows what I'm talking about," as a student named Jacob yawned during our lecture, drawing the attention of the class.

The student, no more than 20 meters away, let out a sound that swiveled the heads of nearly the entire lecture hall. The lounging groan of a hearty yawn, rising from his wide-stretched mouth. The perturbed teacher crossed his arms and stared, eliciting the reaction of a few hushed snickers. Jacob continued that unending yawn, however, flooding what seemed like utter defiance and immaturity across the class to the point it became very uncomfortable. "Am I losing my connection to the youth?" the professor joked with outstretched palms, drawing forth a few chuckles from the class. The tone changed quickly, however, after that awful crunching sound began.

The human jaw is capable of exerting nearly 270 pounds of pressure per square inch. The muscles are immensely powerful, allowing us to chomp through the toughest meat and survive as long as our teeth are intact. It's these powerful jaw muscles that widened that student's jaw into a grotesque, wide oval.

They stretched until a sickening cracking sound created gasps, yelps and nervous whispering throughout the class. We all heard the snapping sound of jaw bone and knew something was terribly wrong. His tormented groan from his impossibly wide yawn was filled with agony, and we watched as the yawn caused a shiver which built into severe convulsions.

The teacher realized this and came to his aid, removing his phone to call 911, but as I watched as his other hand reached upward to cover his own mouth. That pesky little contagious feature of an act meant to keep us alive with oxygen ended up stretching the teacher's mouth beyond what seemed possible under his cupped hand. The hideous cracking sound, followed by the quivering of his head that only the most fulfilling yawn can deliver, was soon followed by a gush of blood flowing down his graying mustache. The teacher's ears and nose trickled red, but his mouth, his mouth began to pour like a waterfall of deep crimson from that massive, bone-splintering yawn.

I rushed out as best I could. The screams now bellowed from the flurry of running students, some covering their mouths as the class fled the auditorium in panic. People were tripped, shoved and trampled as survival instincts kicked in. I jogged out onto the streets of the bustling city and breathed deeply and methodically through my nose, using my focused will to keep my jaws locked closed. I walked briskly away from the screaming, crying crowd that spilled out onto the streets behind me, towards the river's edge and away from the chaos.

The amber alerts soon began rattling phones and delivering messages; unknown airborne contagion suspected, cover mouths, stay indoors, towels in door and window gaps, tune in for further instruction, etc. They had absolutely no idea what this was. They had no idea this epidemic was a false instruction that tricked our bodies, but who could have possibly predicted it? Our entire being is full of fail-safes that keep the toxins filtered, the irrational thoughts contained, the bacteria bombarded by white cells.

We like to think our bodies can't be tricked into self harm, so we trust them. It is hard to accept how easily our anatomy is duped. The next few days of widespread panic revealed just how easily even isolated wealthy couples in their hermetically sealed mansions were susceptible. They would bleed out from snapping jaws due to their own rebelling musculature in quivering yawns of death.

Emergency oxygen tanks were deployed by FEMA to try and keep the fatal contagious yawning at bay. Scientists failed to produce any useful findings aside from it having possibly resulted from an undetectable virus that masks itself beyond detection. Others blamed a mutation within our genes that ended up backfiring, an artifact of evolution. Nothing was of any true help, however, and nothing will help. Practically no one can unsee, unhear, or completely avoid that triggering signal that causes the muscle memory to backfire. People are simply biding borrowed time from the enemy that is their own body, ready to fold open their face with a crack of the mouth, leaving them to bleed to death and to rot.

After that last class a few days ago, I walked carefully so as to not fall from to the effects of custom muscle relaxers I created to protect me from my apocalypse. I walked down to the river to the boat I'd purchased on the pier; my fully stocked blue catamaran I'd spent my bloated tuition money on. I know the domino effect I'd set in place will play out by the time my supplies start to run thin based on the computer simulations I'd ran all semester. I know roughly when the world will be silenced from the chain reaction started when Jacob, who will soon be referred to as patient zero, gripped my pricking handshake in introduction.

I sit now in the warm sun on the water with my solar charged cell phone, ready for the month-long epidemic to play out and to deliver a message for those I selected to survive. I'd share it, but it's just a set of instructions and I'm sure I already bored you, possibly enough to stir a yawn.

SYNTHESIZER

My neighbors hate me and I don't blame them, but when you hear the skull-jiggling bass spill out of my speakers, you feel a few miles closer to god. Keyboards are my life. I have a collection of 42 synths, including some very precious gems, a Moog muSonics Minimoog, TWO Juno-60s and a Aries Modular 300. I had an opportunity to buy an iconic System 35 once, but I'm not rich. It's taken me over 18 years to build my collection. When I was browsing Etsy, Ebay, Shopify and the likes as I do a few times a week, I stumbled upon something that made my heart oscillate like the machine gun buildup up a tightening square wave.

In the 1930s, one of the earliest pioneers in electronics had developed an early synth, the pioneering Mixtur-trautonium that shook the world through radio broadcasts and sound design. It was a large beauty of knobs and pedals on a rack, and was unchallenged for many years aside from one rumored competitor, a man allegedly named Adelhard Klein-Grutzmacher, who according to rumor had vanished at the start of World War 2 and was presumed dead. The listing I stared at was for the Grutzmelodicon, the only rumored synth of his, clearly by someone who had no idea how rare of a gem this was. The price read $150.

I sent an email with an offer of $220, provided I could pick it up that very day, hoping to outbid anybody else responding without tipping the seller off too much. That synthesizer was worth at least $40,000 as described, fully functional and near mint condition, and most importantly, no living soul in recorded history had even seen one aside from in an early sketch. I paced back and forth with my heart refusing to quiet, refreshing my mail app and unable to focus on anything aside from a possible response. When the email came through, "Sure, thanks for the generosity! Come on by, just buzz a few times, I have poor hearing," followed by an address I leapt on my desk and shouted in triumph. I called my bud Z-man and told him to stop by with his truck, NOW. "I'm at work," he responded. "NOW!" I begged and he groaned and gave me 20 minutes to pace frantically.

My bud pulled up his truck, and I ran out to meet him.

"Where's the fire, dude?" he asked, a little grumpy in contrast to my elation. Tim is a large guy, the nice kind of asshole friend, a non-violent but argumentative giant, never afraid to show his annoyance. He also was a synth head and a talented player; I had to save the surprise and show him in person.

"Just help me out, you'll see," I asked to his groan of a response. He flipped me the bird and set the truck rules, he picks the music, I pay for gas, and this better be good. I nodded, and we took off to the address in the middle of nowhere I'd input on maps as day began dimming to dusk.

After nearly 40 minutes, the GPS signaled we'd arrived, and my legs tingled with the high of stretching from the car seat and onto the dead grass of a neglected lawn. The place was very run down but fairly large; it had clearly been a lovely 3 story home perhaps twenty years ago. I knocked on the door, then remembered the email. I buzzed hard several times to make sure I was heard. I nearly buzzed again when the door opened a sliver to reveal an elderly man, gaunt and hunched, with very large hearing aids under wild, white hair. He looked to be over 80, and he said "Come in, right this way," with a very strong German accent.

We entered, and the smell of mold and decades of dust crept to our senses. The house was very sparsely decorated with ancient cabinets and a couch from the 60s. Old photos were scattered on the wall; family members, soldiers during the war, a young pianist playing. It was hard to see clearly as the dark house seemed one massive shadow, pierced sparingly by ochre beams of light from dusty windows. "In the basement," the man creaked, and I felt nervous, despite the holy grail of a score that awaited, and the fact my large friend was with me. The stone basement walls emanated a chill that seeped into my clothes as we descended, but soon we were on the ground floor and there it was, cover removed, in all of its glory.

"Holy sh—" Tim began, and I had to slyly kick his shoe, shaking my head to signal that the value of this item might not be known by the current owner. The look on his face spoke volumes though, he knew exactly what we were looking at. We proceeded to haul the heavy vintage synthesizer upstairs with quite a struggle, loaded it in the truck, and returned to the older gentleman to thank him and pay him. My friend's eyes bulged in absolute disbelief as he saw me count out $220 to hand the seller for the treasure we'd loaded under a bounty of blankets. I thanked him kindly and Tim and I drove off.

"Is this SERIOUSLY what I think it is?" Tim shouted, unable to contain himself, now out of hearing aid range. "For TWO HUNDRED AND TWENTY DOLLARS!" I smiled, gloating.

"The only one in this beautiful world, the only one viewed by anyone aside from that man in over 60 years." I smiled broadly, unable to contain my joy; I felt like I'd won the lottery. We hauled it into my place a few hernias later and marveled at it, the ornate woodwork, with decorative carvings that looked to portray mythological tales. It looked to be black mahogany, and it was stunningly beautiful. I pushed it to a wall by itself, studying the onyx black keys that took the place of the white keys of traditional keyboards. The knobs looked to be ivory or bone, others gold, the parts of this thing alone were worth thousands.

The stain on it was elegant, near black with a gossamer sheen; not a single scratch on the pristine surface. I found the plug and crossed my fingers and toes. I could tell Tim did as well, and we plugged it in.

There was a staticy crackle as the vacuum tubes inside came to life, and it seemed to drain the ambient noise of the room, lit warmly by an orange light hazing up from the gaps of black keys, highlighting their form. We high fived like children and I pressed a black middle C key down to release a roar of the gods. The bassy tone was fat and crisp, clearly some tremolo on the modulation that was years ahead of its time. I reached over and turned the familiar looking knob that read "RES" and the sound crisped into a haunting, saturated tone.

"Jesus, this is unreal, may I?" Tim asked, eagerness in his eyes. I would have all the time in the world to figure out how it worked; no instructions existed for this beast of a synth. I agreed, rose from the chair and studied the cabinet. I noticed some unsavory symbols on the device, but it was German-built during the onset of the second world war, I guess it was to be expected. "How the fuck did YOU get this?" he half-jokingly commented, playing a spine shivering chord that could make Giorgio Moroder cry. Tim was quite talented, but it was the synth that made everything sound perfect, like an audio MSG so rich it made you hungry for more. I looked at the date etched into a brass label near the base, a slightly sour taste entering my mouth, Auschwitz, 1941.

Despite all implications, I just had to let this slide as this was the one and only Grutzmelodicon. Tim played around first, sating our eagerness to hear the incredible synth's cosmic ballad. It had three oscillators and some technical developments that weren't released until decades past its conception. I made him get up so I could play despite his severe protest.

The power of the synth made me feel like a god in command of a siren's song.

When I was done playing, I looked at my phone to see 32 missed calls. Someone was trying to reach me; there must be an emergency. I felt panic and scrolled through. Work, mom, friends, work mom, friends, they were from multiple days. It was only Saturday but my phone displayed Wednesday. I tried to figure out what was glitching and asked Tim what time it was. He looked distraught, sweating heavily and clearly confused.

"What the FUCK!?" he shouted, clearly distressed and confused as well. "This can't... Is it WEDNESDAY!?" He looked horrified, as I'm sure did I. I thanked him and turned off the machine and showed him out. I rushed to the computer to email work and begin damage control, still in shock. The amount of lies was immense. I explained my phone was stolen in a mugging to my boss, and he seemed satisfied enough not to fire me yet. A long series of apologetic texts had me mostly in the clear, but I was so starving and exhausted I collapsed almost directly after.

Thursday I ate the largest breakfast possible; a cheese steak, eggs and bacon, a fruit salad, coffee and orange juice. I got to work, head hanging in shame and all apologies for the fabricated force majeure I'd described in the form of a mugging. At lunch I housed a burger, fries and a soda and a milkshake, but I was still hungry. I felt like there was a nagging tapeworm inside that was stealing the nourishment from my massive meals. That day I left a bit early, eager to get to the phenomenal yet brooding instrument, and I was shocked to see Tim's truck in the driveway. He was at my door, arms tucked in his armpits, clearly in an anxious state.

"Dude, I got it, alarm clocks," he said, something I'd been thinking earlier that day. Set an alarm and avoid any possible trance-like side effects like we'd both experienced.

"I was thinking the same thing," I explained as we eagerly scampered inside and over to the dark synth born in the dark heart of the war. Before we started, I suggested something physical in case our hearing was affected. Something was disturbingly hypnotic about it, but we needed to play with it, to hear that complete sound that exists nowhere else in the world. I asked how we could make sure to be aware of the time aside from sound, stumped. We stood there like showroom dummies for a second before Tim came up with it.

"Delivery," he said in revelation. "They buzz the door, and we leave it open so they can enter in case we can't hear." I agreed, satisfied, and I flicked on the toggle that made the black keys glow from the shadowy cracks between them. I played a bassy low E# and tried to inhale so the rumbling vibration didn't take my breath away. I patched some cords in the rack, and I blinked, rubbing my eyes. The cords felt fleshy, slimy and looked like slick intestines. I watched as they quivered from the vibratory bass. The all black keys of the piano began to appear like the long teeth of a charred skull; the rack's ports like eyeless sockets oozing veins on a macabre, monstrous face.

Almost immediately after that chord I felt a hand on my shoulder causing me to jump. I spun to see the melting face of a skinny, naked man, dripping meat from a peeling, blackening skull in a violent torrent of blood and leaking gore. I screamed and the fleshless face screamed back. Quivering veins writhed on the form that began blurring as my eyes teared up, and when I blinked again, I saw a frightened delivery man, backing to the edge of the room with our meals in plastic bags. I got Tim's attention, and he was as horrified as I, the fear on his face spelling out he'd seen something nightmarish as well. After a moment he seemed to be back in reality, and we paid the nervous delivery man and turned off the instrument. We ate in absolute silence for ten minutes, also swallowing our fear while plotting.

I finally stated that we shouldn't play it until the weekend, that it seemed to somehow suck time. How he had just sat down to play a few notes when our food arrived and an hour had passed. We'd both had nightmarish hallucinations, and both agreed that this instrument was the cause. He asked to play just a little more like a junkie begging for a fix, but I said he needed to leave and he did, although begrudgingly. The look in his eyes was pure loathing. I half expected him to beat me to death, and an arpeggio of twitches wrinkled his hateful face. He walked away in silence, got in his truck and peeled out loudly, drawing neighbors to windows. He was gone in a bitter cloud of burnt rubber.

I scarfed down the food but was still starving and I stared at that mesmerizing vintage synthesizer as you might a tender pork roast. It was so perfect, so elegant, so satisfying. My fingers danced upon the ornate woodwork. The juxtaposition of Greek mythos and Nazi soldiers carved into the sides of that electric Lucifer beckoned me. Those beautiful gold toggle switches: I knew deep down just what had been melted down to create.

My mother called, breaking me from the spell, and I answered to her tears. There had been an accident, my brother was in the hospital with a fractured skull, she'd been trying to reach me for days. He'd been violently assaulted by a man with a crowbar. I called out of work the second time that week, but I had to be by my brother as he fought for his life.

I arrived to my tearful family, comforting them all and staying by my brother's side, trying to ignore the visible dent in his bandaged head. It was a horrible tragedy, but it brought me to my senses a bit. I was now focused on everybody's well-being and not once did I think of the invisible limits that synthesizer had pulled us across the past week.

After two days, they announced surgery was needed and we should go, but the prognosis was very positive. I returned home, keeping my brother in my heart and thoughts on the long drive back. It was 8PM when I arrived to find Tim's truck in my driveway, the lights in my window were clearly on. "You motherfucker!" I spat, fuming with rage.

I kicked my slightly ajar door inward, noticing the scratch marks on the lock where he'd busted in. I stormed over shouting with rage, but began coughing from a heavy stench. Rot permeated the air, and I needed to cover my nose with a folded sweatshirt in order to get to my keyboard room. Terror assaulted me as I slowly approached those black, back-lit keys. Tim's clothing, wallet and cellphone were strewn across the floor near the crowbar he'd broken in with. It struck a dark chord in me.

It smelled like a corpse had been rotting for weeks in the coffin that was now my music room, but there was no body. I stared at the sticky black trail of decomposition that lead to that death machine, the Grutzmelodicon and the strange carved vents on its base near the floor.

A few fingernails rested in that putrid, black liquid decay, a few fillings from his past dental work, a few tufts of his recognizable curly hair.

That was all that it had left behind. I know I need to get rid of it. I can sell it for a small fortune and buy dozens of rare synths, I'm sure. I can finally quit my job and move to a new apartment that smells so much better. I can meet another best friend with a shared passion for synths. I can do all of these things after I play it one final time.

TODAY'S THE 20TH ANNIVERSARY OF BILLY'S DISAPPEARANCE

There are dark, dense woods in my hometown that were the location of a series of police investigations when I was a child. I never told anybody what I experienced there, aside from the very abbreviated version I told the police 20 years ago today. I need to write what happened on September 3rd of 1998 in Walpole, New Hampshire, in the hopes that it might finally fade from my memory.

My best friend Billy and I were always getting into trouble.

We'd raid the thrift store drop-off boxes for electronics and CDs, we'd shoplift candy from the dollar store and run like the devil when chased.

We were delinquents, both with single mothers and the destined-to-fail mentality of knowing we weren't getting a shot at college. We were the have-nots, and we were fine with that. Just before the first day of school, Billy called my house phone and told me to come over, and to bring a flashlight. He lived just a 12-minute walk away, so I headed out after grabbing the red plastic Eveready from the garage.

I soon climbed his small house's creaking wooden steps and knocked on the screen door. Billy opened it, beaming a wide, mischievous smile under his long, greasy hair. He motioned for me to enter with an arm that looked comically skinny in an over-sized Judas Priest T-shirt, clearly his older brother's. He led me to the ratty, plaid couch that stank like cigarettes and spilled beer, and we both sat. He looked up at me with focused hazel eyes that beamed with excitement over his freckled cheeks. He clearly had a big fat secret to tell me.

"C'mon out with it. What's up?" I finally asked.

"Remember Sarah Benton from third grade?" He asked with a sly smile.

"Yeah."

"Remember how she went missing the last week of school?"

"Yeah, so?"

"Sarah Benton with the $20,000 reward for her whereabouts?"

"Yeah, yeah, yeah, of course, just spill it," I huffed.

"I found her backpack."

"Bullshit" I replied, but Billy just nodded his head slowly without breaking eye contact.

He reached behind the ratty old couch and pulled up a green backpack. It was filthy and stained and it stunk like mildew. I felt nauseated watching as small worms and pill bugs squirmed along the zipper of the smaller pocket, and I knew before even seeing the cursive name tag that read 'Sarah', it was really hers. She'd gone missing after chasing after her dog that ran into the forest. The whole town had searched for weeks, but nothing was ever found. It was a year later, and we all knew she was dead, but this was the first actual lead.

"Holy shit, where did you *find* that?" I asked, feeling the buzz of excitement at the mystery.

"The woods near Mr. Peter's place," Billy said with a conviction that worried me, "We're going to go get that reward today."

Billy stood up, then entered his brother's room. He returned after a few minutes holding two walkie-talkies, and he tossed one to me.

I nearly dropped it, surprised by the weight. "Just in case," Billy said, and I just nodded, attempting to appear brave in front of my best friend.

I'd seen the dozens of "Missing" posters over the year with that big, bold 'REWARD' on them. I knew that $20,000 would go a long way.

We soon were off, walking on the side of the road and talking about game systems and sneakers we'd spend the money on. We veered closer to the drainage ditch when the occasional truck zoomed past, spraying asphalt and chugging out black smoke. No more than 15 minutes later, we arrived at a barbed wire fence covered with those bright orange "NO TRESPASSING" and "NO HUNTING" signs.

I followed Billy as we slipped between the barbed wire and entered the thick woods. It was far too quiet and dark in that forest. It was a sunny day around 3 PM, but it looked like dusk in the immense shade the tall trees provided; it was uncanny. I could barely see any gaps in the many-layered leaves of the canopy. Nearly all outside light was blocked out, and I felt the temperature drop.

"Here," Billy's voice called out, "This is where I spotted it after a deer jumped the fence."

Billy switched on his flashlight and pointed it at a patch of exposed dirt wriggling with worms and beetles. The patch sat just before an archway of low-bending trees that continued into darkness. I wanted to turn back, but something powerful tugged at my curiosity to the point I couldn't even look away from the black void ahead. It was hypnotic, like a hallway framed by arched branches leading into shadow.

"She must be in there," Billy spoke in a muffled voice. I clenched my teeth and watched him step in and nearly vanish before I switched my light on to see his dim form turn to face me. I could just make out the silver sheen of his eyes reflecting the cold beam of my flashlight, and soon my feet followed after him.

I felt a vibration in my skull as my teeth began chattering from the chill. Each step forward, my flashlight's beam somehow seemed to shrink shorter in the dark path, barely able to even illuminate the bending trees at my sides like bars on a cage. I was only a meter behind Billy, but the beam just barely lit his white sneakers, the rest of him cloaked in shadow before they too seemed to vanish in the blackness.

Then I felt something cold and wet brush against my arm.

I am well aware that fear and a child's imagination can present hallucinatory experiences. My shrink told me that over and over before I stopped going, but I know what is real and what isn't. I felt a bony hand wrap around my bicep and squeeze hard, causing a sharp, sudden pain. I screamed out, aiming the flashlight's impossibly short beam over, barely making visible white, finger-like branches bending in the wind.

The beam of my light reached mere feet from the bulb, and every hair on my neck stood on end as I watched the shadows drink the light up the faster than it could project. Then Billy spoke.

"D-d-d-do-d-d-do you see it?" Billy stuttered in an odd, wavering voice.

I always had poor vision, being far-sighted. My eyes strained to focus. I actually *felt* something closing in, but I saw absolutely nothing, just the beam of my flashlight stopping dead on those finger-like branches that swayed in the frigid breeze.

"See what?" my voice came out a meek whimper, and then I heard a branch snapping followed by horrible laughter.

It was Billy, giggling quietly at first as if he was trying to control himself but was unable. His laugh grew louder and hysterical. I then felt something moving closer to my head, inches from my ear. Billy's laughter cackled and spat, rising in pitch into a shrill, explosive howl.

He sounded lost in a psychotic fit, half laughing and half shrieking.

"Billy," I called out nervously, then shouted, "BILLY!"

There was a sudden silence.

I smelled the rancid stench of death and decay and then felt a heavy breathing. My heart pounded in my chest as I raised the short beam of the weak flashlight slowly upward, and I saw Billy's contorted face, framed by his wild, matted hair in front of me as that deep, vibratory breathing blew the hairs on my neck. I was paralyzed with fear, and I'll never forget Billy's twisted expression as he stared at whatever stood over me.

His eyes were wide, unfeeling and somehow changed, as if washed in ink. His drooling mouth hung agape in a hideous grimace like a large wound, bending his jaw. Both his mouth and eyes stretched wider and wider until I could hear the tendons creak and wet pops of muscles tearing within his jaw. His shaking right hand reached down slowly then grabbed his left wrist.

"D-dooo you seeeeee it?" he asked in a drawn-out way that would haunt me for decades.

His fingers clenched tightly on his arm, dripping red where his fingernails punctured the skin. I watched in reeling horror as he then snapped his forearm down at a 90-degree angle, accompanied by a grotesque, loud *crack* of the bones. I stumbled in shock, nearly falling.

His screaming laughter brimmed with absolute insanity as he then inserted his fingers deep into his eye sockets, gouging the plump orbs out as if to remove what they'd witnessed. I heard a low clicking as something large and very long moved past me on my left, and its fuzzy shadow erased Billy from visibility before meaty ripping sounds joined his shrieking laughter.

I ran back through the dense darkness, unable to tell which direction I was heading. I couldn't see anything, but I heard those deep, buzzing clicks just behind me as I ran. I sprinted faster than I'd ever run in my life until the beam became brighter and the faint details of the trees at my side came back into view. I finally exited that tunnel of those arm-like branches, hearing the scuttling of multiple sets of feet following close behind me. I didn't stop running until I was back at the barbed wire fence.

I screamed out to Billy until my throat was raw and hoarse. I repeatedly tried the walkie-talkie, but only heard static. After nearly an hour, I ran home with salty tears streaming down my face. I sprinted into my house, telling my mom to call the police, that Billy was missing in the woods by Mr. Peter's place and someone or something had taken him.

The responding officers questioned me about the thin, branch-like bruises on my arms before conducting a thorough search of those dense woods over the following week. They found his walkie and flashlight crawling with beetles, but nothing else. Neither Billy nor Sarah were ever found. Every night for 20 years that horrible laughter has echoed in my memory, and every night I've prayed they never are.

DOWN A SIDEWALK CELLAR

My cell phone wasn't involved when I fell into the metal grate tonight.

The black doors buckled inward beneath me during my walk back from the convenience store two blocks from my apartment, a deep fear that has always lingered in my subconscious. I always avoid them, but a couple walked on the side closest to the street and I stayed to the side near the shops after I'd passed them. I was thinking of how soon I could get away to see my family for the holidays when the ground gave way beneath me. My stomach rose to my throat as I plunged into darkness.

My ankle rolled to the side upon landing, and the screaming pain of a sprain left me shouting obscenities. I was in complete blackness, and I realized the metal doors I fell through were closed. I climbed the steps and pushed and then pulled with all of my strength, but they weren't budging. The sound of metal clattering startled me, and I froze, my hand pressing hard over my mouth.

I was pretty sure this was the basement of a restaurant—there were a few on this block—but I recalled this being the one that shut down last year. I removed my phone and used the screen to reveal a narrow chamber with shelved pots and pans that looked decades old. I limped back up the stairs and tried the door again, but it was not opening at all. I turned my screen once more to the racks of old kitchenware and began coughing from the ancient dust in the air. I tried to call my roommate, but there was no signal down underground. I was already alone, afraid, and in pain when my skin raised small bumps as I heard a wet clapping sound coming from the next room.

It was the sound of slapping and then sliding, like something was dragging itself along. I quickly put my phone away and slipped into a gap in the metal racks of pots and pans, trying to be as quiet as possible as that dragging sound grew louder and closer. The nightmare of my situation grew as it approached, soon merely a few feet away when it stopped. I stood there, pressed hard against the old cement wall with cold metal shelving against the side of my face, for what felt like an eternity. Whatever was here was only feet away and wasn't moving.

After what felt like an hour, I eventually faced the fact that I had to do something, and I removed my phone slowly and turned on the screen, illuminating a face at my feet, staring up at me.

He was clearly dead; it was an older gentleman who I'd seen on the block a few times. He was bloodied and butchered, both of his legs were missing, severed mid-thigh, and his arms had deep slices as if he'd been hammered by a meat cleaver or a machete. The expression on his pale face was one I hope to someday forget: absolute terror fixed in his wide eyes and his mouth in an awful grimace. The revelation that this man had likely been recently butchered left my heart pumping quickly in my chest; whoever did this was likely going to return. I frantically rushed to the cellar doors and pounded and shouted for help with all of my might, but they refused to budge. I faced the hall, now trailed with blood, that led to the next area of the basement and started walking, realizing the only way out was in.

The coppery stink of blood mixed with the smell of mold and water-damaged wood, an odor nauseating and dense. I held my shirt over my nose as the smell grew with each step into the adjacent dark chamber. I entered and pointed my phone screen at the dark shapes lining the walls. There were dozens of forms sitting upright against the room's walls. They were bodies, wrapped in black plastic trash bags and duct taped closed.

A massive square hole sat in the center of the room, and I approached it, tilting my phone inward to see an ancient stonework pit hazing into unending darkness, a wall-less infinite well that had to be at least hundreds of years old. A strange odor wafted up from the opening: the out-of-place smell of ozone. I took a penny from my pocket and dropped it in to gauge the depth with total fascination, not hearing it land. I limped to the door-sized opening in the wall to the next passage, and that's when I heard the slam.

A door closing was muffled but audible from upstairs through the wooden beams on the ceiling. The floorboards above me creaked toward the next room. I heard muffled talking, a man speaking then silent for long gaps; he was likely on the phone. I could barely make out some of his words, but the ones I caught were "I'm sure," "alarm," and "I'm checking." My heart nearly stopped as I heard that strange sound, a droning hum so faint I thought I had been imagining it, but I wasn't. The sound was coming from directly behind me. I didn't have to look to know it was coming from the hole.

I heard a set of keys jingling from outside that door, and I panicked, running to the edge of the room, realizing I was trapped and whoever had been storing the corpses of the people sitting propped up on the walls was coming. There was absolutely no place to hide, and in a grim realization I knew I could either join them in death or try and pretend to. Desperate measures led me to rip the plastic off of a horribly butchered, sinewy man whose jaw had been chopped clearly through. I dragged the cold, heavy body over to the hole and teetered it in before dressing myself in that plastic and propping myself in the corner in his place. I held my breath as the door opened and heavy footsteps descended the stairs and shuffled around on the cement floor.

Time crawled to a halt as the sound approached. I was sure any second a blade would split my skull or sever my limbs, but I played dead, the horrific fumes of human decay being huffed like nitrous out of the trash bag I occupied with my slow, steady breathing. A short burst of static was followed by a gruff voice in panic stating, "Oh fuck oh fuck oh fuck, he might have fallen in," and then a loud smack of a body on creaking wooden beams followed by the raining patter of liquid, some which drummed loudly onto the trash bag covering my face, nearly giving me a heart attack.

I heard a deep grunt from lungs far too large, then a sickening ripping and more liquid falling in beads to the cement floor around me.

I then heard the dragging from the walls to the center of the room and I realized the bodies I was hiding among were being dragged into that hole, and I had no choice but to run or join them in that pit. I took a few quick breaths of the rotten air, ready to jump onto my swollen ankle and run, when that voice spoke, a familiar voice.

I scraped into a wall in the overwhelming darkness but kept running forward with the throbbing pain of my ankle as I heard a deep huffing and snorting from behind. I tripped onto the steps and scampered up them on all fours as quickly as possible to the door that, by the grace of all that is good, was not locked. The dim streetlight through the windows illuminated the dark, stripped interior of the old restaurant, which was being renovated. Plaster, paint, and debris sprawled about.

I looked back only once, but I saw it, and I no longer believe in god. No god would have ever made that thing, no matter how evil or angry or deranged. The fractals of teeth like a crabeater seal in thin, rippling skin on a face on a head twice the size of mine. Those large eyes with lids that blinked shut like an "X." That twisting tongue that flailed around as if a separate being under the cavernous hole of a nose.

The sickening, musty, yet sweet smell of centuries on its skin.

I ran faster than I ever have in my life, despite the excruciating pain storming in my swollen ankle. I unlocked my building door, scurried up the stairs, and tried to still my shaking hand enough to unlock my apartment door. The process was somehow sorrowful, something terrible was eating me up, but I couldn't place a finger on what, as my sole desire was to get into my room and lock the door behind me. It was only once inside I realized it. Only after that horrible screaming from outside my street side window curdled my blood. It was only then I realized that in my panic I'd left the door that led out of that cellar unlocked.

WHAT'S WRONG WITH MY BABY?

Sarah was born two weeks premature, an emergency C-section after three sleepless nights in the hospital when a tangled umbilical cord threatened her and her mother Rachel's welfare. She was a healthy baby, and after a few days by my wife's side, the new doctor handed me Sarah in the hall and instructed me to take her home while they treated Rachel. Rachel had suffered from some complications from the ordeal and needed to stay at least a week to recover while being monitored. I missed her at my side and was new to the whole parenting thing, so I called out of work this week to take care of the baby. Sarah slept in the car seat on the way home with me, and I finally felt we were all going to be okay until I first saw something odd.

As we neared our driveway, I heard the gargled grunting Sarah was making and looked over to see her arms and legs miming a running or climbing action, which I'd never seen a baby do before. It might have been cute, but her bulging eyes and sneering, tiny mouth looked twisted and strange. Unease stirred in me as I told her, "Almost home, sweetie," and reached over a gentle palm to brush her forehead when her growl intensified and she strained her neck back, pushing her softball-sized head firmly back against the car seat as if to get away. I withdrew my hand and parked, carrying her indoors as she writhed violently.

She seemed very agitated, but that was just the beginning I carried Sarah inside, a bit overwhelmed trying to care for a newborn on my own. She was so small yet so heavy, so expressive with the miserable faces she'd make; she had an intense

"

stare like she was perpetually shocked and filled with disgust. It was creepy, and the more I tried to console her, the more she looked like she was furious. I placed her in her crib and went online, letting her rest as I researched what I could do. Message boards explained they were unable to communicate at this age, people said they often screamed endlessly, but she wasn't screaming; she only seemed to be brooding, growling, and making those awful faces. I eventually nodded off, exhausted, and when I came to, I nearly had a heart attack.

I lay on the couch, my slivers of closed eyes opening to reveal a bald silhouette hovering over me, jarring me with shock. My wide, fearful eyes at first had no understanding of what I was seeing until that gurgling groan, bassy for the infant, began to build and raise in pitch, higher and higher until it reached a horrible, blood-curdling scream directly into my face. Sarah's tiny body fell forward, falling with her tiny arms plunging deep into my gasping, open mouth, stabbing into my throat.

I immediately gagged, pain flashing from her weight against my tonsils and uvula, and I pushed her away to remove the tiny, intrusive arms. Shock was plastered on my face, and in the cold shadows of the night, I could see Sarah was smiling. Not a happy baby smile, this was a menacing smile full of hatred and impending suffering, only far more nightmarish with that toothless grin that seemed far too wide as her skin stretched like wrinkled latex.

I looked over at the crib, completely unable to understand how she'd even gotten out. I picked her flailing, kicking body up, checking the dry diaper as she grumbled, and placed her back inside the crib with a bottle of warmed formula. I fetched the square of Plexiglas I'd purchased for my photocopier Halloween costume and placed it on top, weighing it down with old college books that weighed nearly their cost.

Confident this should hold through the night, I curled back on the couch to get the sleep I so desperately needed. When I was startled awake again, however, only half an hour had passed.

Sarah was making vibratory groans, seemingly too bassy for her small frame. She was standing on the kitchen countertop, visible as only a silver-lined shadow, backlit by the cold moon from the window.

The glint of a knife blade showed in her miniature hand, and I jumped up to race over to her. I flicked the light on and watched in confusion as her facial features seemed to relax back into place from stretched and relocated positions like a terribly contorted rubber mold had been released. An eye had eased back from the top of her head, one from her ear, the mouth, a quivering set of drooling lips that flexed as a hole over the muscle and bone of her chin on its return to below the nose. Her dangling arm without the knife twirled slowly like a cord relaxing in more than three revolutions. The other gripped the knife handle with white knuckles.

I glanced over to the crib, to the snapped Plexiglas, and blinked unbelievingly. I approached, looking into Sarah's wide eyes and snarling lips as she breathed heavily from flaring nostrils. I was on the verge of cracking but reached up slowly to try and coax the knife from her. A whir of silver cut the air, forming a red line on my middle finger below the nail.

Drops formed from the cut, so I grabbed an oven mitt and placed it on, reaching slowly again, and Sarah plunged it into the mitt before I could even react, and I watched a red stain swell on it with the accompanying pain. I'm a problem solver by nature, and as I swatted a handled wooden cutting board at her, the knife stuck in, jutting through cleanly, and I yanked the blade in the board away from her. The hatred on her face was beyond any I'd ever seen, but I tossed a towel over her and slung her over my shoulder, carrying her back to her crib.

Sleep deprivation had really taken its toll on me at that point, but sleeping was clearly not an option. I'd had eight cups of coffee in the past twelve hours. I watched as black liquid spilled from the crib, trickling in a waterfall oozing from the bars, then growing on the floor like a puddle of oil, but I wasn't going to clean it up now. When the sun had finally risen, I called Rachel for help, but that just confused things further. She kept telling me to go to sleep and that Rachel was fine, but she clearly didn't know how hard it'd been. Rachel wasn't making any sense, saying Sarah's sleeping like a newborn, but I could see her standing in her crib, twitching and making her face wrong as she stared at me from behind the bars.

BLACKSKULL'S LAIR

As a recent nine-to-fiver in NY, my day started like every other. A rushed exercise routine, a breakfast burrito microwaved, followed by reading emails while scarfing it down. I showered while planning my day, including my dreaded four p.m. meeting with the dour-faced project manager, and I was out the door in thirty. Commuters clogged the arteries of sidewalks, wet from the drizzling rain, and I reached the subway to find it closed for repairs. I cursed the MTA, hoping to find a taxi, and to my relief one was idling right there. The light was on, so I ran over and hopped in to direct the driver to my office. I smelled something pungent and chemical, and I asked the driver to crank a window. That was the last thing I remembered before waking up.

My head throbbed as if from a hangover, and I was laying on a smooth, plastic-like ground somewhere dark and cold. I lifted my heavy body from the textured floor and tried to figure out what the long passage I was in could possibly be and how and why I was there. Gaudy faux stonework walls reached high to an arched ceiling of mock brick, which all seemed to be made from airbrushed fiberglass, shiny with enamel clear coat. It was dim, lit only by a fake torch wedged into a holder on the wall that illuminated the corridor in an orange glow. I had no idea where I was, but it looked like part of a some massive theme park attraction. With no warning, a deep, gravelly voice boomed through a hidden speaker from the ceiling that made me jump.

"Welcome to Blackskull's Lair. You have been chosen to wander the walls of wasted wanderers in this lethal labyrinth.

You have nothing but what you came with, and in order to survive, you will need to face ghastly abominations unlike any you have seen. There are hundreds of perilous pitfalls and torturous traps, bloodthirsty beasts and murderous mad men. There is only one path out, and it has yet to be traveled. May your death be delivered duly and your screams silenced swiftly if you fail." A feedback squeal followed the end of the transmission, and I stood, blankly staring down the long passage.

I waited a good minute for a punchline that never came, and then I clapped; this had to be some elaborate prank or some outlandish game show *Cash Cab* type of situation. I was impressed by the production value—this would have been hilarious—but I had to be at work. I listened to the echo of trickling water and heard some distant clacking sounds of unseen mechanisms. I tilted my head up and smiled while speaking to the empty hall. "What is this place? That was great," I said, but my fingers fidgeted. I removed my phone and checked the time. Five p.m.? How had I missed the entire day? I then saw the numerous missed calls.

I flipped through my emails, frantically responding that I was sick in a desperate act of damage control and then realized the date listed was wrong: it read the 19th. I began panicking; I'd lost two days. I walked down the torch-lit passage, slamming the base of my fist in frustration on the smooth, solid wall that jutted out molded stonework of a mossy hue. My GPS was offline, but my phone worked, at least.

I knocked on the solid surface and wondered where I could be with growing unease. This place felt far too complex to be a prank and too cruel to be a game show outside of possibly Japan, which watered the seed of worry in the back of my brain. I shouted, "Where am I?", and it echoed through the passage. I walked down the hall until reaching the edge of where the fake torch's plastic-flamed flashlight could illuminate. I nearly jumped when I heard some deep, ragged breathing, and I glanced behind me to the source, seeing a flicker of a shadow in the darkness. "Whoever is doing this, it isn't funny, and it is very illegal," I tried to firmly state, but the lonely reverberation of my voice was the only answer.

I backtracked and removed the decorated flashlight from the fixture, and memories flooded back to fantasy games I'd played as a child before I'd been teased about them. I continued down a cobbled path, noticing detailed, airbrushed accents that seemed almost artful.

There were fake cracks and rubber mushrooms drilled into the corners, stains and moss airbrushed in great detail that seemed a labor of love.

After a few minutes of appreciation, the feeling of being trapped returned with a reeling claustrophobia.

I nearly tripped as I stepped on a movable stone panel that sank down from the weight of my foot, causing me to drop the plastic torch to the floor. As I bent to fetch it, a clicking startled me, and a metallic screech rang in my ears as rusty steel spikes over a meter long speared outward from the walls just inches above my lowered head. I screamed, knowing just how narrowly I'd avoided being impaled, and I touched the rusty skewers, confirming they were very much real.

I crawled quickly past the spikes down the long, surreal corridor. My eyes teared as I jumped back to my feet and frantically dialed 911. I spoke to the dispatcher in a voice as calmly as I could as I explained my situation. "I've been kidnapped and trapped in some sort of maze with deadly traps. No, this is not a prank call. No, my GPS isn't working. No, this is NOT A PRANK." I relayed information as they asked for specifics I just didn't have, and then I heard freakish, labored breathing from just behind me. Crawling under the spikes that now slowly retracted back into the walls, I then saw that horrible and very real face.

It was some deformed creature that looked nearly human, but the head was a twisted, abstract clump of flesh with butchered features.

The thin, sinewy body was just bone and knotted muscle, and he wore only a filthy loincloth and belt. He carried long, metal swords that extended from inside the flesh. They seemed affixed to his skeleton.

Where eyes should have been were folded flaps of mangled skin, and the rest of the face was a twisted mess of lumps and slivers. The nose was missing, a pulpy pink cavity, and the lip-less mouth flashed lengthy gums and jagged teeth that seemed more from an injury than a birth defect. I yelled as the thing charged toward me, and I ran down the long hall toward a three-way fork.

I caught my breath, squeezing the plastic base of the fake torch as I looked back at the flailing thing chasing after, swinging those steel blades, which clacked loudly against the sturdy walls. I faced a fork that split the path into three distinct wooden doors with symbols painted on them, then jumped as that exaggerated, sinister voice spoke through the speaker once more. "Beauty is in the eye of the beholder. Better choose quickly. Brad B's close, friend."

Brad B… That had such a familiar ring to it, but it took a moment for the suppressed middle school memories to flood back. Brad fucking Bastino, the spoiled bully with that asshole smirk, the newest sneakers and anything he ever wanted. He'd shove me hard into lockers and call me horrible names that the other kids picked up on. He punched me after school, threw my book bag in the trash, and spit in my hair more times than I could count. I remembered dying inside nearly every day; I only survived because he'd eventually discovered another target. Was he stuck in this maze, too?

I tried to quickly understand the three strange symbols painted in drippy crimson on the doors: a crescent of a moon dripping lines, a sun with extended rays on the top half, and a cross made of other crosses. That thing rapidly approached, lashing wildly with those sharp blades with strength I assumed stemmed from the needle marks on the veiny arms near that familiar tattoo. I then noticed the scars from stitching on the grotesque face and temples, and my jaw dropped with the realization.

This thing chasing me was human, born an upper-middle-class kid I'd known. This thing was Brad Bastino; he'd been carved and stitched into this freakish remnant of a man. This thing closing in had been my tormentor back in middle school before he targeted that childhood friend I fell out of touch with. Before he targeted Billy.

THE REASON HART ISLAND IS CLOSED TO THE PUBLIC

My father would often talk about his brother Ronnie with great fondness. These past years laid up in the hospital, my father had shown a longing for closure with Ron, who had gone missing in the eighties. He was presumed dead after serving time at Rikers for a murder during a botched home invasion. I'd begun the journey to bring my father closure, nothing more. A series of online searches of his records and calls to the DOC led me to learn of his labor on Hart Island just East of the Bronx. It was on this island that he dug graves as part of his prison work program from which he had vanished, assumed drowned, nearly three decades ago.

In my research to find more, I read with growing interest about the enigmatic Hart Island, cloaked in secrecy in the Long Island sound.

Hart Island's dreary history spanned centuries starting with its initial "sale" from the Native Americans. Spanning the past few hundred years, the island housed prisoners from the South during the Civil War, the mentally insane, and then tuberculosis patients in the 1800s, and drug addicted youth in the 1970s. Programs were phased out through different generations, however, and the only remaining inhabitants were the dead. It's estimated nearly a million bodies were buried in shallow, mass graves under the dismal, gray soil.

In the 1800s, the infamous Blackwell Lunatic Asylum on what is now known as Roosevelt island began to experience overcrowding, and the overflow of inmates were sent to receive care, or more accurately negligence, at sister facilities on both

Randall's and Hart Island. A few dozen women were unaccounted for when closing, and despite a series of trips by law enforcement to comb the island, they were eventually registered as drowned. The funding vanished and the asylum closed before Hart Island's conversion into a rehabilitation center for troubled teenage boys, most of them court mandated and drug addicted. After an unacceptable number of them went missing as well, the program, under thorough scrutiny, finally closed in 1976.

Since then, the island has served as the final resting place for the countless souls with no easy access to next of kin. Those bundled on the streets in blankets during snow storms, those displaced from mental health facilities due to lack of funding, those runaways found with no ID, and hundreds of stillborn children. Once their life is extinguished, devoid of immediate family, the John and Jane Does are boxed in pine and ferried over to be stacked in bulldozed trenches, buried and lost in time.

After a number of families sought closure through the years, the Hart Island Project was created, bringing awareness and limited access to ferry a few family members to visit their lost loved ones on the restricted island. The process involved negotiating with the department of corrections due to the tax-funded burial site where inmates assumed the roles of pallbearers. As I researched the tragic stories in an attempt to help my father track his brother, for the first time, I became truly aware of the plight of millions without the safety net of a family. My father's quest to find Ronnie became my own, and I set about contacting the city with the help of this recently opened program to visit Hart Island and find closure at the potter's field.

After filling out the online form, waiting for weeks, and finally booking an appointment, I woke early to jump on two subways, then a long walk before the gaudy orange ferry came into view. There were only four others, a quiet but pleasant group of us who showed IDs and handed over all electronic devices, cameras, and cellphones, metal jewelry, and the likes. A nervous wind mingled with the brisk air as we set off along the channel before the flat island grew wider on the horizon.

There was a gazebo available for the two "tourists," those without family on the island who had to stay behind. Only a pleasant elderly woman named Mildred joined me as we followed the officer to the directory to locate the general area where our relatives were buried. I saw a tuft of grass shiver in the wind or perhaps from a rodent but continued following the guide as he led us over to the gravestone that my uncle shared with hundreds of others in that dreary ground. I swore the ground seemed to be moving, and I walked back, looking closely, when a white light flashed in my head.

A piercing headache dug into my skull unlike anything I'd ever felt. I shook my head and wiped my eyes as the pain punctured my temples. I staggered and collapsed onto the dusty earth, clutching my head in my hands, when I heard something that sounded almost like a whispering. I watched the guide up ahead turn and notice me, then begin to approach in order to help when the soil separated and collapsed under my feet. I was plunged into darkness, almost ten feet down, and I then heard the breathing.

I heard the squirming sounds of worms and smelled the pungent odor of decomposition as I lay in the darkness, holding my aching head.

Breathing heaved from rattling chests and teeth clicked together around me. Licking sounds and rasping breaths steamed musty odors in my direction as my eyes fought to adjust to the dark cavity in the crumbled ground under dozens of rotted coffins. I heard yelling from the guide, but it was muffled and distant, somehow farther away than it should have been. I flinched as cold, moist fingers of thin skin over knobby bones wrapped around my arms and began to pull me deep into soil that felt like equal parts rotted flesh and mud.

I tried to scream, but my throat filled with falling debris. I sunk into the earth, flailing wildly in an effort to escape, but dozens of skeletal hands and teeth yanked me deeper into the soft mud. I heard them now, whispering, crying in shaky voices, and begging for me to help them. They had messages for me to deliver to loved ones, hidden money they needed retrieved, and vengeance they sought me to fulfill for them. Their murderers' names and addresses, their boss who fired them unjustly, their rage and jealousy of their siblings and greedy friends, instructions to finish the violence they'd started, and other more innocent pleas were etched into my terrified mind as they breathed out their final requests.

The creaking voices wheezed demands, begging me to find their lovers by name and deliver messages of forgiveness, to make sure their children got the money the murderous husband stole before killing them, to bludgeon the man who stabbed them; it was overwhelming, and my head screamed with pain. The voices of the dead became a horrific din as I was pulled downward by countless desperate, rotted hands. As a convulsion shook my body, I realized my lungs were unable to find air; I was suffocating with the mud and flesh of the countless dead, and I began to slip into darkness.

I felt hands pulling on my arms in the sockets of my shoulder, a burning heat that swelled as I was guided through the mud. Fingers reached in my mouth to remove dirt before my lungs were pressed into by heavy hands that pained my ribs. I gasped a breath of air and found myself on the ground, staring at the gray sky as two starlings soared overhead. I had been pulled out and was back on land and had received CPR, which saved my life. In the following hour, I was placed in the visitor's office in a modest medical area. I was examined and given some tea as well as a blanket, but the taste of rot and mud was stuck in my throat.

They said I'd fell in a deteriorated stack of coffins, an unfortunate accident, and the waiver I'd signed explained the hazard was an unfortunate possibility due to the wood rot. After I finally returned home, I read up on ocular migraines and hallucinations that explained away bits of what I heard and felt, but not all. The dead spoke to me in countless requests, the need for vengeance and messages for loved ones when I was under that ground, and my unease became a shiver when I decided to search online. The names were all real, the addresses as well.

I now have a list of tasks the dead demanded, and I'll tend to them all, once I see my father in the hospital first. It's my burden to tell my dad on his deathbed that Ronnie knows he framed him, and he's clearly not willing to forgive.

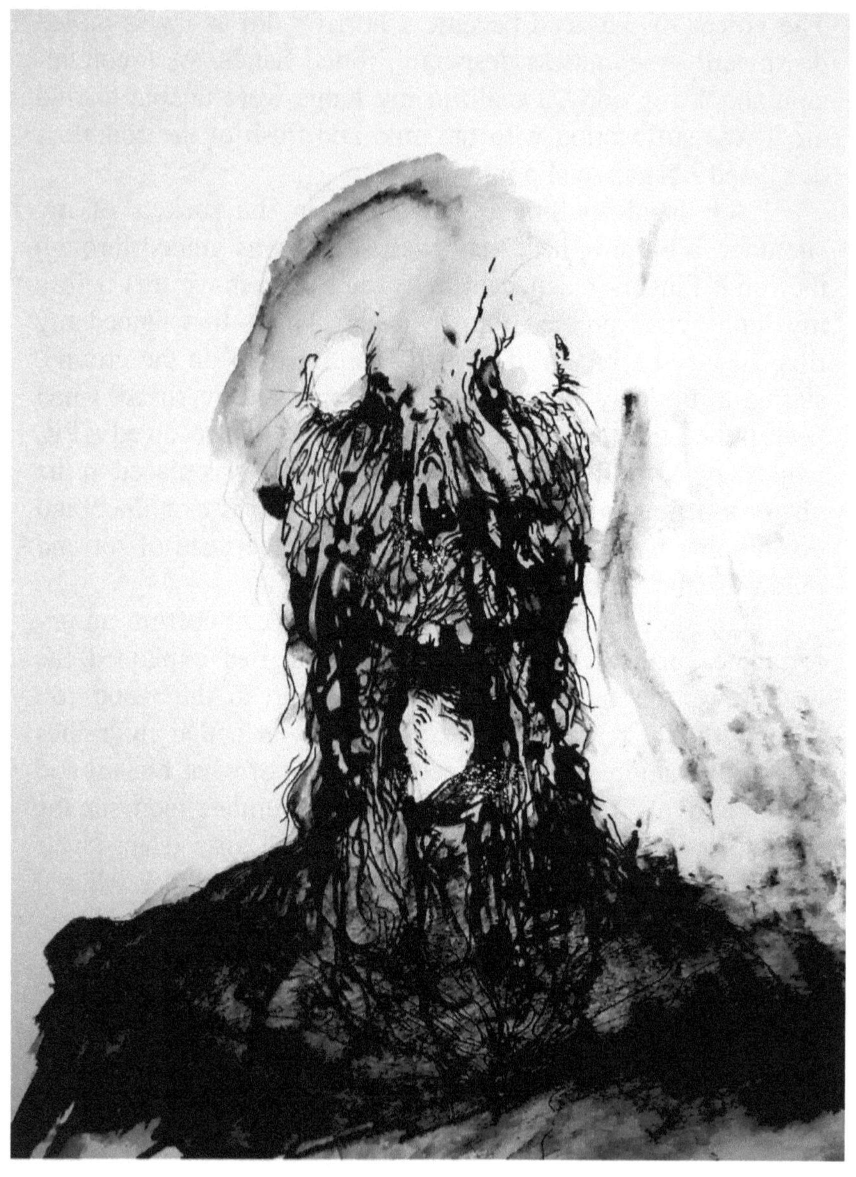

THE COLD LADY

I work as a CNA at a retirement home, and I love my job. After completing a twelve-week certification program, I was with a respectable facility's residents through many times, both the good and the bad. There were a few folks that were depressed, a few that were forever grumpy, but most were delightful people with beautiful personalities, and each and every one of them was a part of my family. Some required more maintenance than others, especially those with dementia, and nobody seemed to have that worse that a woman the residents referred to as The Cold Lady.

Most might tell a clever joke pertaining to their day, or at least a pleasant hello, but the Cold Lady, a long-time widow named Mary, would only speak the word "Cold," her hands clasped around the elbows of her long-sleeved shirt, eyes staring through a wall into the distance, sulking and miserable. I always tried to offer her blankets, occasionally placing one on her lap, but she never wanted them and would toss them to the ground. After her mind fell ill, it was as if she was trapped in a loop, her only connection to other people being that single-worded complaint about the temperature.

Residents occasionally complained about the cold, of course; as muscle mass deteriorates, people have less insulation, and the chill passes through them far more easily. I always made sure the heat was at least at seventy-one due to the consensus of the residents, and Mary's room was eighty-one nearly year round, yet only she complained so endlessly about the cold. She wasn't violent, and she didn't have any meltdowns like some of our more sensitive and needy residents, but it was always a bit creepy to both the staff and the neighbors on her floor when they'd pass and she'd just stare at a wall and whisper, "Cold," in a slow, detached manner.

As the winter chill cooled the nights, freezing water droplets formed in window corners, and I readied myself to hear a good, few dozen earfuls of the word "cold" from our dear Cold Lady, Mary. I made sure the thermostat was set accordingly to accommodate all of the residents as I made my rounds on the floors last night. All was well after dinner, after the movie they'd requested, and after I'd made my rounds checking vitals and assisting the nurse in distributing medication. Each floor went seamlessly, and I looked forward to possibly leaving early, but of course luck would have it there was some commotion coming from Mary's floor, a sound that creeped me out, something I'd never felt in my two years at the retirement home.

At first, I thought it was a dog, some high pitched, yapping sound from down the hall. I took the stairs, which opened up to the tiered balcony and allowed us to hear commotion from any floor (a big help to us CNAs to assist a resident in need as soon as we heard them).

I heard it from afar, getting louder as I climbed the stairs to her floor, and realized it was a frantic yell. I approached the hall in shock, each one of the patients with severe dementia was pacing anxiously, looks of fear and confusion on their faces from hearing Mary "The Cold Lady" barking out words from behind her closed door.

She was screaming, almost coughing the words louder than I thought her vocal cords would allow as she chanted, "Warm! Warm! Warm! Warm! Warm!" from behind the door. It was surreal, the other patients stumbling in agony at her shouting voice, which was beyond disturbing, and I tried to help the others back to their rooms as Mary's horrible yelling erupted into a scream of, "Hot! HOT! HOT! HOOOOOT! HOOOOOOOT! HOOOOOOOT!" I paged the front desk to request security, but nobody was answering, which was even more unsettling. I decided I needed to calm Mary or there was no way I could control the situation. I walked to her door, knocking loudly and twisting the handle to find it locked. I removed my keys, unlocked the door and opened it, and nearly dropped my phone in shock.

Mary was staring out the wide-open window, screaming louder than I'd ever hear a senior scream before. She turned her head to face me, and I saw a horrific smile and fervently excited eyes that nearly bulged out of her head. She stared at me and screamed, "HOT! HOT! HOT!" faster and faster, as if playing the childhood game and on the verge of being found. I approached, hoping that perhaps this was some strange game she'd decided to play this evening, but I abandoned that notion after my first step toward her, when she suddenly collapsed to the floor with a loud thud and a shattering crack of glass.

I ran to her side, kneeling to take her pulse, finding none, and checked if she was breathing, which she wasn't. Mary had a DNR (do not resuscitate), but even if she hadn't, I'm sure I would've let her be after I paged the nurse. Clasped firmly in her hands was a cracked framed photo of her late husband, and childhood sweetheart, Jeremy on the night of their wedding nearly fifty years earlier. I stared in awe at the blowing drapes of the open window as I went to close it. There, in the freezing, winter wind, sat two gold wedding bands, stacked together on the windowsill.

THE CONDUCTOR

People often ask me what I do. Lately, as a slight smile sneaks onto my face, I explain I'm a conductor. They act impressed and intrigued, asking more before their raised eyebrows slowly scrunch in confusion as I turn away to ignore them and their unanswered questions. I'm a conductor of opuses of unfathomable beauty, but my works are only truly heard by me. I composed my latest nocturne last night and conducted it this afternoon in a busy intersection in Midtown.

The horn section is often neglected, so I made use of David's from his unassuming black vehicle, double parked near the coffee shop.

I'd followed David for a week, noting his remarkable timing each morning as he fetched his coffee and returned to the car he then drove to his bank downtown. It's amazing to discover that a work schedule is a promise of attendance at specific places at specific times. David was always punctual, as often are those who value their jobs more than the welfare of others.

The homeless man had a different type of job by far, but he played the sleigh bell chime of coins shaking in his cup as he stopped Jacob and his small son with one phrase that resonated. It was this homeless man that I'd slipped $40 to, hidden folded inside a one dollar bill, also containing a Post-it Note. The note promised the same for the next five days if he'd stop the man in a green suit walking by with his son by calling out, "Jacob, is that you? It's Mark," his childhood friend he'd pretend to be, opening a window of distraction.

The symbols, the metal circular trays of those pies of pizza for the fake office party I ordered, were deployed, and their delivery man was so utterly terrified of dogs. The howl of strings barked furiously by Ms. Daulton's formidable large rescue dog on its morning walk, passing by at the same time to create a commotion and ensuing distraction. Jacob's son was also deathly afraid of dogs, and it only took him edging back from the crowded sidewalk scattered with bacon crumbs and into that open street. David's car barreled down the road, distracted by the pizzicato sounds of viola plucking emergency alerts from my well-timed texts based on a simple mistaken email so similar to his own to his boss.

The child entered the path of David's car, spilling the small body to the street to meet both abrasive asphalt and heavy steel and tire with the deep bang of the timpani. Skin was scraped violently from the skull and blood spilled in a heart-pumped spray onto tar. My fingers danced to cue the falsetto screams of the choir on the sidewalk as pedestrians howled the notes of my composition. The song's crescendo arrived in perfect time to my dancing hands as the oboe's wail signaled the ambulance, unable to save the crushed body of the small child in the street.

David had chosen to deny the loan, and we were unable to afford the treatments. Since he effectively prevented her shot at life-saving procedures, he'll now know clearly how it feels to take a life.

That was nothing compared to Jacob, the man who'd decided to terminate Amy and her health insurance based on the "growing liability" to his company, knowing very well what he was doing. He took Amy from me, and his child has been taken from him.

This was my second composition, and I have a few more yet in store. The doctor who chose to ignore the symptoms Amy insisted were real until the cancer had already spread. Her father, who claimed she didn't help him so why should he help her, despite his fortune. The list is longer than seems right, so there are a few beautiful compositions I look forward to conducting in the somber key of absolution in the next few weeks. If you pay close enough attention, you might hear my work being conducted.

BAG BOY

Bagging groceries may sound like a dull job, but bills need to be paid, and right now, my design skills are apparently not up to par with the class of 2017. I work three nights a week and close up the supermarket after, as I have for the past two months. The night manager usually does this, but he's been dealing with a newborn, and I have little to do lately so felt obliged when he asked, promising an hour of overtime. Since the shop is close by and in a well-lit and relatively safe part of town, I never felt even the slightest unease. Earlier tonight, however, I saw something wrong with my reflection, and my world began drifting deep into darkness.

I helped the slow yet incredibly charming Mrs. Carmine load her groceries into her hatchback and then returned inside to help the cashier tally up and close out. I looked longingly at the black glass window to the outside, eagerly awaiting kicking off my shoes and relaxing with a movie. The bright lights in the supermarket created a mirror effect, and I stared at my slumped self, aware of how miserable I looked, and tried to smile. I returned some stray cans, swept the area, and headed out to fetch the carts. The nipping chill of winter had arrived earlier than expected, so I rushed through the job, hearing a strange wailing of the wind that sounded somehow alive and creeped me out. I ran to fetch the last visible cart, jogging it inside to warm up.

The cashiers all settled up with the closing manager and headed out as the lights dimmed. I said my goodbyes, mopped the floors, and looked at the view through the black glass to the now-vacant parking lot. My reflection was visible among the aisles of cans and preserves behind me. I turned my head and saw my reflection do so with a trail effect that was unnatural and off. I blinked, disbelieving, and stared at my reflection intently, realizing something was different. It was like a double exposure, and in that moment, I realized someone seemed to be outside, mimicking my exact motions while looking in.

I nervously stared toward the hidden form, covered by my own bright reflection in the black, mirrored glass. I slowly approached the large pane as shivers climbed my neck. As I stepped forward, the form followed my steps, getting closer until I could just make out a hairless head and a shadow of a face within a streetlight-lit sliver on the silhouette's edge. I walked slowly over to the pane, watching my reflection trail a slightly misaligned form from outside just feet away, separated by that tall pane of glass. I edged closer and closer until my face was inches from the glass, my own backlit shadow finally revealing the face only inches away, and I screamed.

In the blackness of the entrance sidewalk in front of the empty lot stood a man with no hair, eyes, or nose, just creases as if his head was Silly Putty that had been pressed into repeatedly by a wide chisel above a black, lipless mouth. Bony hands extended down from a tattered winter coat beneath a green apron much like my own that was covered in dark smears I immediately knew was blood. The figure outside fidgeted its wiry fingers as if in anticipation, and I realized in absolute horror that it was waiting for me.

I ran to the doors to lock them, the figure mirroring my run with my reflection, and I stopped dead in my tracks, realizing the automatic sliding doors were the only thing separating us. I froze, then began stepping backward away from the door, sighing in relief as it retreated as well. I remembered Tom, the guy I'd replaced when I'd started who just ditched work and never came back one evening. I realized that Tom's apron was likely the bloodied one it wore. He never had left without notice, heading to his friends in San Diego after all. I began to freak out, the dire situation hitting me heavy as falling bricks. I kept backing up, away from the door, the form mimicking my body's motion as I removed my phone from my pocket.

I dialed 911 and reported an intruder while hearing a horrific, tongueless yelling from just outside. Eventually, sirens cut the sound short. Red-and-blue lights flashed, and the figure appeared to be gone.

The rescuing officers entered while the static distortion of police radios chirped from their shoulders, their weapons drawn. I raised my hands and explained what happened to the furrowed eyebrows of skepticism.

Despite their squints and sneering, I filed the report quickly; they seemed in a hurry to get on their way. Eventually, I walked them back to the entrance, looking at the large glass window and seeing our reflections lag slightly, both the responding officers' and my own. I didn't follow them, I warned them as best I could that there was something dangerous outside, but of course they only saw their reflections and ignored me. They instructed me to get some sleep. I tried to show them, but they simply refused to believe me.

The taller officer threatened me with arrest when I tried to hold him back, and I let go, hands raised in submission as I watched them leave. Their two wavering reflections nearly matched their every movement, but I knew there were three of them out there. I only ran when I heard the screaming and cracking sounds from beyond the sliding doors. I ran in an Olympic sprint through the stockroom doors and into the manager's office. I locked myself in and barricaded the door with the swivel chair, breathing quickly with my heart pounding.

After what felt like hours, more sirens arrived. The EMTs had clearly been called to the scene with an additional set of cops. I'm just waiting in the dark recesses of the stockroom now, trying to ignore the almost human grunts and yells from the darkness surrounding the office. I've bagged enough today without joining those poor officers outside on the zippered black plastic delivery to the coroner. I just wish my reflection on the glass windows of the office stayed still instead of inching ever so slowly out of alignment toward the office door.

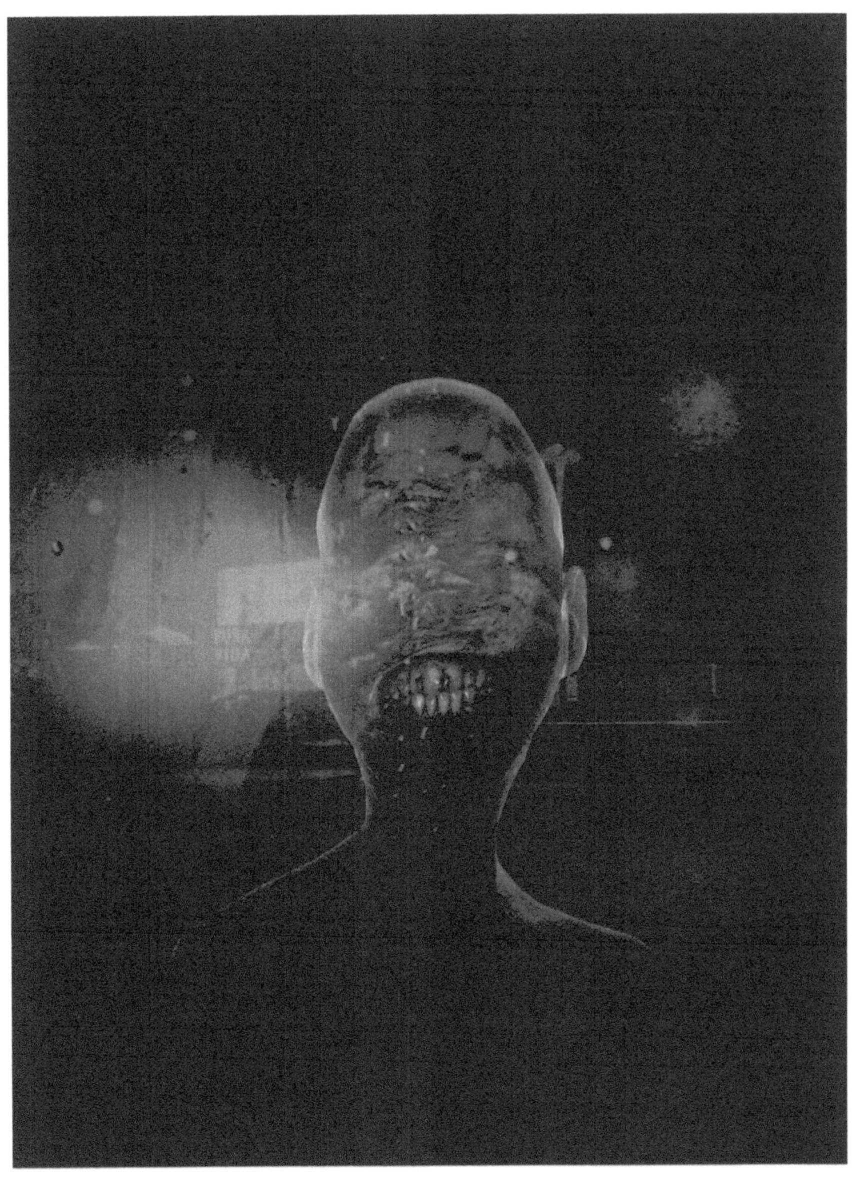

STOP ME IF YOU THINK YOU'VE HEARD THIS ONE BEFORE

Stop me if you think you've heard this one. A man walks into a bar. The next day, the same man walks into the same bar. The next day, the man walks into the bar again. Rinse, repeat. I know, you heard that one, but you haven't yet heard why. You haven't heard the story that leads to that bar, the man seemingly blurring out of focus and into oblivion.

Anything to try and wipe the replaying nightmare from his every waking moment.

My fiancée and I were inseparable, that cutesy fresh-in-love couple that makes you sick. A deluge of sweet nothings, shared plates at meals, kissing affectionately and holding hands. We were that annoying couple, and I won't apologize for that. No more, though; now I shovel food down with my cap low, a sliver of my jaundiced, bloodshot eyes glowering with brooding misery. It was the day I proposed that this nightmare began.

I'd been saving for months and wanted casual, so I told her to meet me near my office for lunch. I "tripped," ending up on a knee and shocking her with the ring. She said yes as tears glistened and her voice fluttered, and my eyes naturally joined in, blurry and wet, as we embraced. I will never forget the look in her eyes when she said it. I'll never forget the look in her eyes when she bled out on the sidewalk, her face an abstract, exploded wound.

We'd spent the day in the park before heading back to the apartment. We made love as if the world was ending, yearning for each other in a passion that was truly alive. We talked about dreams and about children. We made imaginary plans, picked baby names, suburban communities to raise our children until college, world travels in retirement before assisted-living homes and grouped plots in a lovely graveyard near the woods. It was a playful game partially based in reality with a sense of humor I felt only we so closely shared. We eventually left for a celebratory drink at a bar to meet her friend and spill the beans about the proposal. The drinks spilled next, then the blood, and then tears.

A congratulatory set of shots loosened us up, and Claire headed to the dance floor. Soon after, a large, older, goateed thing felt free to try and rub up on the smiling, dancing woman who was my fiancée. I let my face redden until the anger launched me to my feet, she was clearly unwanting of the attention, so I stormed over to push that thing aside.

Nasty words were exchanged, glares and threats, but it eventually left the bar.

My fiancée felt violated by that creep, so she talked to her friend, Maggie, who was clearly a bit drunk. She needed to head outside with Maggie for some fresh air, and I settled the tab. I headed out to hear my fiancée cursing and saw that piece of shit forcing her against a truck, undoing its belt buckle under that disgusting gut. I saw red and grabbed the cigarette butt holder and swung it hard to smack its vile head, and it then fell. Threats boiled from that scum's mouth, and I held my fiancée, consoling her and wiping tears as we left to my car.

It was clearly aimed at me; my fiancée leaned and called Maggie, who was still puking by the bushes. A loud gunshot spilled out of my wife-to-be's beautiful face, opening it in a horrible wound that painted me red with spray. I tried to hold it closed; she was dead instantly, but my mind refused to accept it. The truck drove away before any action could be taken, and I tried CPR and mouth-to-mouth on what was left until the police pulled me off and her body was placed on a stretcher. They covered her up, and that was the last time I saw her. My beautiful wife that would never be because of that thing I refuse to refer to as a man. That thing that kept me coming back to the same bar every day for the past eight months, not to forget, but because of something that Claire had ripped off its neck in that struggle.

It wore fake dog tags, clearly not military issue, some online order that the piece of shit used to try and lure victims by lying about its loyal service. I'd found them in the shrubbery outside as they took Claire away; she'd torn them off as that trash tried to violate her before taking her life. She wanted me to find the name of the monster, the name I'm withholding to avoid sentencing once this has been published.

The police never found it due to no effective leads or clues, and it had known it hadn't been found yet. Once the smoke cleared, that thing headed back to prevent any chance of being discovered. My corner at the bar was strategically placed for the angle of the mirror, and after months of planning and patience, I saw that truck pull into the back of the lot. I saw that fat fuck, hat low and face down, walk slowly across the parking lot to the bushes where it had occurred, and for the first time before closing, I stood up, dropped two twenties on the bar, and walked to the bathroom to fetch my bag from the drop ceiling.

In order to make it stick around, I'd gotten a replica set of tags with that name, soldered to a chained cement block I'd buried one night after closing. This bought the time needed to slip on the hoodie and track pants that were in the bag and hop out the bathroom window. I parked my electric rental car with replaced plates on the side to seamlessly slip inside, and I started it. I drove over, launching the taser darts deep into its back from close range. I squeezed the trigger for far too long, but nearly a year of waiting made it impossible not to. I smelled the foul odor of shit, and I punched that unconscious face before loading it in the rental. After zip tying the arms and feet, I used a ketamine injection to keep it from moving on the ride.

My heart raced as I drove on the highway. My nervous wide turn out of the lot seemed to draw the attention of a cop, who lingered close behind, but I followed every rule in the manual, and soon he picked another potential drunk driver to follow. I safely cruised to the outskirts of town where I'd been paying rent in cash for a storage locker. I picked one with low visibility in the back but used the crate and dolly to conceal the transport of the cargo from the car and into the storage unit nonetheless. I lugged it inside, slammed the door, and unboxed it. I placed it in the steel chair with a hole in the center, the chair that I'd welded on the square steel plate on the floor. A smile slipped onto my face for the first time in eight months as its eyes groggily opened.

Fear has a funny way of showing itself. The attempted threat of anger and hostility soon fades once the mind realizes it will not help.

Bargaining takes its place on the table; offers of fortunes and savings spill from its lips, apologies and remorse. It mentioned its family, wife and children, and that only fueled the rage. The family I was supposed to have, the wife it took from me, the children I would never meet, and the X-ACTO blade came out.

I used it to do a few unmentionable things from the source of that fecal smell and the song of screaming lit the space alive, landing softly into the insulation and soundproofing I'd installed. I spilled the blood-clotting suspension on the area stained red and brown and looked that thing in its eyes, making sure it knew exactly why it was there. It already knew when it realized those dog tags were not moving, but I wanted it to see just how much restraint and forgiveness it would receive from me as I pulled out the illustrations I'd worked so hard on, showing what to expect.

The first thing it took was my fiancée's personal space, and I let it know how that felt first in the form of the tapeworms I poured down its throat, spilling fluids to the ground. I made a few lacerations on its body, no more than ten inches apart from another, and I let the maggots play. The eyes spoke volumes; expressions of horror I had no idea were even buried in our darkest recesses of our minds jumped forth as it screamed that song my ears delighted in hearing. IV drips of the solutions I'd researched that would keep it alive were jammed into veins, and I let the personal space invading continue for a week after crushing the vocal cords.

I called the tow company to report its truck to be towed, claiming it neglected for over a week, and it was after that I'd returned to the bar the next day. I sat with the locals, sipping beer and whiskey, trying so hard to look my somber, miserable self. I was never going to be all right ever again, but every time I emerged from the bathroom, binging the live stream of the tortured thrashing of that thing in its chair, I had to think of my stolen wife in order to conceal any change in mood.

After a week, I returned to the storage unit to feast my eyes on the disgusting mess on that metal plate on the floor. Massive, festering sores spewed maggots and pulpy tissue, and to my delight, some bone was nearly exposed. I made sure to bandage it appropriately so it wouldn't bleed out. The eyes delighted me; they begged for sympathy, which was hilarious. I actually laughed out loud as I exclaimed, "You thought it was over?!"

The second thing it took was her dignity as it attempted to sexually assault my fiancée. This part was not enjoyable to me, but it was very vital to teach a proper lesson to the subhuman thing before me. I used the deodorizing agents and ventilation system I'd set up as the lye, coffee grounds, and baking soda seemed to lose their effectiveness. I made sure it looked and fully understood what the splintered wooden phallus was for and why there was a hole in the chair. I switched on the motorized mechanism under the seat to thrust into the thing on the chair. I looked deep into those wide eyes that tried so hard to explode outward and bleed to death, but there was more to learn still. I swapped the IV bags and refreshed the powders and filters and returned to the bar the next day on schedule.

Sally was a gruff but kind waitress, and she was there the night it happened. The night it came and took everything, and she always poured me some free shots. I no longer wanted them but forced the sour well whiskey down in order to maintain my standard presence as the broken man drowning his sorrows. I engaged in some conversation about a fictitious job I no longer had and drank into the night until closing as usual, spitting out shots secretly and trying not to look too happy as the week came to an end. I drove to the storage unit, fighting off a smile I unleashed at those tormented, insane eyes of that thing on the chair that smelled nearly as foul as it should. Gaping wounds were gnawed through, skeletal portions of arms and legs showed gangrenous craters of pus and bone. It tried to plead for death with those eyes, and I was here to tempt it, but I had other designs marked down on the list.

The third thing it took was her beauty, and this was the part I'd been waiting so eagerly for. Claire was beautiful inside and out, a flawless gem one sees only in fleeting dreams among the clouds in seraphim form. I removed the gag and sliced through the tongue quickly to prevent talking. I used the blowtorch on the railroad nail I'd ordered off of eBay until it glowed white, the heat beyond what my gloved hand could bear without the steel tongs. I slowly moved it toward the mouth, singeing hairs and blistering red the lips with heat as I pressed the glowing spike over the tongue's severed tip to cauterize the wound.

I used the blowtorch for the rest, slowly melting away the bubbling lips and shaved hairs to fuse the skin and the skull in a melted horror that would terrify Ed Gein. I left the eyes to make sure the full-length mirror let it see as I removed the scalpel and split its face open to spill out the mess from inside that skull I chiseled open. I left the brain; I wanted the trauma on that to be inflicted by recognition of what it truly was. This rotted, split, deformed thing was as close as I could get to reflecting its insides, and it was then I patched the wounds and pulled out the camera and rolled out the flat screen with the feed of the live webcam to broadcast. I replaced the IV drips and freshened the container, and the live-stream began.

You may stumble upon a site showing a constant display of truly incredible special effects, a monster so horrific it makes you ill.

You may see your reaction in the top corner as you grimace, vomit, and spew forth horrific insults during your observation. Every sneer, dry heave, curse, and laugh is heard and seen by it. I hear them too whenever I am in private, in the bathroom or on a lunch break from my new job. The video may cut as I occasionally force feed it via the tube, change bandages or scrape rotted flesh, but it will be on longer than any syndicated show. I've heard the same disgusted screams and the gurgling attempts of its communication dozens and dozens of times before, but I know that they will never get old.

THE SQUEAL

I have been hearing it for the past week. A high-pitched squeal, almost like a baby's voice but a bit fainter. I've been hearing it in evenings mainly, keeping me up at nights and occasionally waking me from my sleep. None of my neighbors have kids, and it sounds like its near me on occasion, but if I look, nothing will be there. Because of this, I've been not only creeped out and confused but also exhausted.

A few days ago, I explained the problem to a cynical friend, Brian, insisting he hang out at my house until it happened. He ended up crashing on the couch, and neither of us heard it at all that night. I can't begin to explain how not only frustrating it is but also horrifying to hear something that only comes when you are alone. Nobody believes you, and it happens when at your most vulnerable. After some online research, I learned of tinnitus and prayed this could be the cause. I made an appointment and counted the hours in the days until then.

The doctor was friendly and gentle with the otoscope, placing the black plastic cone into my ear. He ran a few tests using headphones with varying beeps of different tone, panning from ear to ear. In the end, he frowned and explained my ears were perfectly healthy aside from signs of an old ear infection that did some minor hearing damage, likely from my youth. He shifted the conversation to talk about auditory hallucinations. "It's not just psychiatric patients who experience these," he said with an a stern voice, trying to ease my concerns before raising them. "They could be signs of brain stem lesions, tumors, or strokes."

He scheduled a CAT scan for the following day to be sure no impending medical risk was at hand.

After an hour in a creepy metal tube with knocking sounds, I was presented the news that nothing out of the ordinary seemed to show. My brain appeared to be perfectly healthy, and though they expected me to be relieved, I was not.

"Does this mean I'm crazy?" I asked the doctor in desperation, and he assured me it was proof of nothing but a healthy brain. I returned home, frustrated and bewildered, and I spent the rainy evening reading online about people hearing noises before night fell with no solid leads.

And then I heard it. It was loud, right outside my window it seemed. A squealing, guttural wailing, the lungs too small to be larger than a possum. Chills crawled up my back as I slipped on clothing and went to my second floor apartment window. The patter of rain rattled the glass as I peered out into darkness. I saw nothing but raindrops and was just about to head back to sleep when I saw the form.

The raindrops were being displaced by something that was not visible, as if a glass sculpture dangled below my window, frozen mid-climb to the building's outside wall. It was roughly the size of a turkey but very difficult to make out the form aside from the fact that it was clearly there. Whatever I was seeing bent my ability to rationalize it, and I was overwhelmed with chills. I removed my cell phone from my front pocket and opened the window to snap a photo, but it was too dark to make out. I turned on the flash and took another, but even then it didn't register with the motion blur because of the falling raindrops. I then switched to video and recorded a few seconds,. Raindrops exploded on the invisible, breathing form, which gave view of its shape. It then shocked me when it screamed that awful cry, jarring the phone out of my hands only to bounce off of the unseen thing before tumbling down to crack on the sidewalk below.

I gasped in shock and scrambled backward, nearly falling, then quickly clawed through the kitchen drawer for a sharp knife. I stared in horror as raindrops fell onto the apartment floor. There was a trail of water slowly approaching me; whatever it was, it was now inside.

Panic swarmed in my head; I was now phone-less, and that thing was in there with me. The water droplets were barely visible, and I could just faintly see where it was in relation to me. I heard some drool-filled, high-pitched wheezing and an occasional squeal as the thing approached me. In a last minute stroke of brilliance, I grabbed flour from a glass jar on the fridge and scooped out a handful, hurling it toward where the thing might be. Shocked that it worked, I now stared at a partially visible form capped with the white powder. It was hideous, like nothing I'd seen, an abomination somewhat similar to a cross between a human infant and a tumorous amphibian.

The face stuck out at an odd, sharp angle, dog-like jaws and no nose; the musculature of its back was excessive along a knobby, tall spine. The thing charged forward with an angry scream, and I jumped back, leaping behind the couch and clutching the cushion tight with trembling hands. The thing crawled, much like a baby would, even faster now in my direction, and I ran over to a broom that was leaning on the wall next to me. I tried to poke at it to keep it at bay. This seemed to anger it more. The thing clung to the broom, then climbed it rapidly, flexing the barely visible, flour-covered legs as it scuttled to my hand. I screamed and instinctively lunged forward with the knife, feeling the force of the small but heavy thing impale itself on the blade where the unseen chest area might be. The thing wheezed a bubbling gurgle, then fell to the ground with a thud.

I tried to slow my breathing and rapid heartbeat as I edged around the thing, fetching the flour once more to sprinkle on the form on the floor. It looked to be breathing slightly but dying. I was shocked by the grisly shape of the lumpy, gnarled thing. I had to move fast with no phone, so I pulled my laptop out and contacted a few friends on Messenger, and everyone just said I was full of shit, drink water, and sleep off the effects of whatever I'd taken, and honestly I would say the same so I can't blame them. My one friend Brian, who lives closest, agreed to come by, so I waited patiently near that oddity, which I covered with a wicker laundry basket, securing that down with a heavy table. The thing seemed to no longer be breathing, congealed flour mixed with invisible blood that pooled a bit past the basket edges. I jumped as the startling noise of the door jolted me out of a weary state, and I buzzed my friend in. From the doorway, he stared in at me with raised eyebrows under a soggy cap and asked, "Where is this so-called creature?"

I led him to the wicker basket, removing the heavy table first and then noticing the large hole. The entire side was mangled as if exploded inward. "It escaped!" I said in anxious frustration, noticing the flour trail smeared toward the window. Brian walked over and stared at the basket and said, "No, it didn't. Look at the basket. It's been smashed inward. Something broke in. Something took it." I followed his steps as Brian slowly crept his way along the wide streak of water and flour to the open window. Of course, nothing was out there aside from my shattered phone, but at least Brian believed me about something actually being there. I shut the window and locked it, doing a sweep of the place to make sure it was really gone before locking up. There was no way I was sleeping there tonight, and Brian offered his couch.

We descended the stairs and walked to fetch my shattered, soggy phone, noticing the milky puddles of flour quickly diluting in the rain. I tugged Brian's sleeve, but he just stood there, shivering in place, frozen in terror. He was staring forward, and I followed his gaze to the large area of water being displaced by the hulking form just meters away, by the unseen beast as large as a muscular and deformed Great Dane that bellowed a bubbling, deep scream before charging toward us. We ran.

We both sprinted from the squealing, invisible beast behind us, dashing into a nearby bar, nearly collapsing out of breath onto the ground. Every patron spun on their stools to face the commotion we'd created upon entering. At first, the bouncer wouldn't let us in as I'd left my ID at home, but I pleaded and convinced him to let me stay to use the pay phone, that there was some dangerous rabid dog chasing us.

Eventually, they let us order some soda and water while we waited, but I'm getting very worried. They close soon, and even worse, it finally stopped raining.

YOU WILL ALWAYS BE MY BABY

Seven pounds, two ounces after thirteen hours of excruciating, tailbone-bruising labor, you were born. Samantha, my child, my angel, my everything. You came out screaming nearly as much as I was, tears blurring from tender flesh stretched beyond limit until I thought I'd rip in two. They always say it'll be hard, but they never describe the deep, burning pain enough to truly understand what's in store. They never explain the frantic urge to get something out that is stuck, lodged inside of you, and not properly shaped to use the door. Nonetheless, you lay in my arms, screaming in your small voice, and as oxytocin flowed, our bond was forged.

My mother had always described my birth as both her happiest and saddest day. I'd been an emergency c-section, nearly hanging myself and killing her after entangling on my cord. She always said it was the happiest because I was the most beautiful thing she'd ever seen.

She said it was the saddest because she'd lost something from within.

She'd lost the infinite wishes and endless possibilities as I grew to meet the reality of time itself. It's a bittersweet thing when you are granted a wish because the infinite becomes a written page, and letting go of "what if" begins to form the reality of "what."

Samantha, you're the same, a bloody, pink, hairless wish, squeaking with screams from exposure to a new and uncomfortable world. You have so much to learn, as did I. So many experiences like teething, the painful itch beneath your gums that you can't quite reach.

The same itch will endlessly torment your body as chickenpox spread throughout the skin, and nothing is worse than an itch that can't be scratched. The itch returns as a rejection of friendship and the fresh sting as a playmate steals your favorite toy, but it only gets worse, my sweet dear Samantha.

You become fascinated with another, a feeling you cannot yet understand is love, and when you reach out in honesty and passion they humiliate you. The rejection feels horrible as a young child, worse than losing that favorite toy to the bullies, but the world ending as salty tears are licked under a snotty nose still can't quite compare to the screaming misery you have in store. You will soon look back to those days in envy, in powerless nostalgia, wishing more than anything to claw your way through time's iron skin back to that simpler, less painful world.

You'd learn what a group of students is capable of, the sadistic tendencies of pack mentality and the brutal assault on your dignity that would occur nearly every waking day. The imperfections of your freckled and pimpled skin, the ugly way you talk, and your bird-like nose fueling their insatiable desire to force you outside of their cliques and torment you. My dear Samantha, they'd call you fat and pinch and punch your jiggling parts in the hall as you lose focus on your studies.

Your will would begin to fold with their insults and your own mind would feed the hatred toward yourself. You'd then start to blame me for even having you, as I did my own mother.

As if by a miracle you might pass your schooling, though the inescapable distraction will have hurt your grades beyond redemption.

Unable to get into the schools you knew you should've been accepted to, the stark reality of a mediocre education would hammer into your shaky will and your weakening bones. You'd see the path forming on its own like a river through a mountain, unable to be altered no matter how many dams you attempt to build. After a humiliating breakup with a boy you thought loved you, you'd realize just how utterly undesirable you truly are, and the voices would echo until they become your own, until you accepted a job you hate, a man you hate, and little by little you'd resign to misery. That's what I'm saving you from, dearest Samantha. I'm saving you from what

I had to endure these stretching decades of choking, endless hell.

I sing a song as I bathe you, but you don't know the words, so I sing it slow. Your skin is at its tender peak, flushed pink with new blood and new life as you struggle, but you are cleaner now than you'll ever be as the liquid drips over your writhing from. I'm saving you from the filth that sticks, the grime and the pain that seeps into pores and courses through blood to stain you. Formaldehyde fills your lungs, silencing your gurgling screams and ending your fidgeting stirs to be with me forever, so know I'm protecting you, Samantha. You'll sit on the shelf by my side, an open book floating weightless with no inked pages of shame, struggle, or strife. You will always be my baby, now and forever, floating in that jar of your second womb by your brothers and sisters.

THE UNFOLDING ROOM

My childhood best friend Brian and I fell out of touch shortly after college, and over the past few years, I'd only seen him through short glimpses of social media posts. He'd been a respectable mathematician at the college in Massachusetts he'd taught at, and though unmarried, he seemed to be generally happy as far as I could gather. A man of math and science, logic and levity, I first thought his account had been hacked into when his posts began to shift from clever musings about scientific pioneers and math-related puzzles to bizarre and almost religious rantings before he disappeared over a month ago.

Brian would typically post comments about historic events of that day, honoring Marie Curie or notifying a very select few about the upcoming Abel prize. His other more casual posts would document wine pairings with dinners and an occasional shot of owls and other birds he photographed as a hobby. His posts were short, witty, intelligent, and always a bit tongue-in-cheek, using double entendres and a few clever jabs at the political or social figure of his choosing. They became cryptic and confusing, however, and people became concerned.

It was as if a switch was flipped, and I'll avoid sharing too much of his private life but will show you a few posts to demonstrate the shift.

September 22, 2017

"Five Room House puzzle, can you cross each wall using a single line?" with a picture of two rows, one with two columns over a row with three shorter ones. One person got it correct after a half dozen wrong, one eliciting Brian's insult that the fellow had "one room short of a five-room house."

October 1st, 2017

"Invention, my dear friends, is 93% perspiration, 6% electricity, 4% evaporation, and 2% butterscotch ripple," accompanied by a photo of a bowl of ice cream on a picnic table with dense trees in the background.

October 18th, 2017

"Personal perfect project." A photo of him in overalls holding a hammer, building a wooden structure, a few pics of him sawing lumber and affixing doors to frames.

November 3rd, 2017

"The Nine Room Paradox: Ten weary, footsore travelers All in a woeful plight Sought shelter at a wayside inn One dark and stormy night. 'Nine rooms, no more,' the landlord said 'Have I to offer you To each of eight a single bed, But the ninth must serve for two." The poem that continued on was from the late 1800s and presented a riddle as to how ten men all seemed to end up with their own room. Two people answered correctly, but Brian didn't reply.

December 7th, 2017

"God hides in plain sight in the fold, everything has been lying beneath the surface, hidden but it's right there," to the response of laughing Dawkins memes and questions of whether he's okay. Some were from his colleagues at university, and it became clear he'd been absent from work for some time, which was disconcerting.

December 11th, 2017

"Seeing an old friend today," with a strange photo that looked like an endless spiral of blurry framed squares descending inward that was a bit creepy and beyond confusing. The replies to the post were mostly from the following weeks, from concerned friends and family asking anyone with information to contact them as well as hopeful wishes from his other friends, even prayers, which normally would have been ironic had it not been for his recent reference to God. There was nothing but silence on his end.

I texted, called, and emailed him, but nothing garnered a response. I just hoped he'd show up soon, perhaps via an apology post after a vacation or on a friend's page who'd found him at a clinic recovering from some existential breakdown or midlife crisis.

That changed four days ago when I received a cryptic SMS message from Brian's number. There was no text, just a blurry pic of a hand holding an open wallet, and chills crept up my spine as I squinted, realizing it was mine, with my driver's license and my credit cards in the slotted pockets.

I checked. My wallet was still in my jeans, and there was no way Brian could have gotten the photo without breaking into my apartment and photographing it in my sleep, which was beyond unlikely.

Furthermore, the wallet was held in front of the sun-bleached wood of a structure I recognized from my past. It was his parents' old barn in Lancaster, PA, where we'd played as kids, nearly two hundred miles away.

Flooding memories of getting splinters from shimmying up wooden beams and falling onto hay stacks to dodge hurled potatoes made me smile. I hadn't been there in over twenty-five years, and the nostalgia pooled tears of relief over my eyes with the realization that Brian was likely okay. I texted him back a few times with inquiries and tried calling but heard no response and grew concerned once more. I finally decided that come the weekend I'd drive down there to try to put my worries to rest.

Skyscrapers grew further apart from each other as the skies opened on the southwest drive. On the road, I planned ways to address him if he'd truly lost it; he was one of my oldest friends, and he had contacted me before all others for some reason or another. Perhaps a stroke had affected his brain and motor functions. I just needed to make sure I at least checked on the one lead I had in case he needed my help.

As the swaying stalks of wheat and corn blurred past through the framed car window, memories mixed with a déjà vu I'd not felt in ages.

The last time I'd been this far into Pennsylvania was at his father's funeral just a year after his mother had passed, and though Brian had been all smiles and polite conversation, his eyes had shown he was devastated by their loss. As the GPS guided me down windy roads and past Amish territory (a culture of which neither Brian nor his parents shared), I began to recognize the curling perimeter of trees and rolling lawn of their farm and residence.

Sure enough, Brian's car was in the driveway with his college bumper sticker as well as a very tall stack of wooden planks twelve feet high and maybe eight deep. My mind jumped to the "personal project" Brian mentioned along with his photo of holding a hammer on his Facebook page. I felt a peculiar unease as I knocked on the house doors and windows, finding them all locked before heading to the barn. The barn door was slightly ajar, and upon glancing in, I was dumbstruck.

Within the walls of the vast wooden interior of the barn stood a newer wooden structure of nearly equal size. It was as if Brian had decided to build a slightly smaller barn inside of the barn, with ceilings, sturdy walls, and flooring as well as one single door on the left side.

Hundreds of schematics and plans littered the floor in stacked and crumpled piles, frantically crinkled and scrawled onto with frenzied notes. Words and numbers were scribbled down in equations and formulas I can't pretend to have understood, fractions, angles, and spirals drawn hastily across large pages of newsprint. I called out Brian's name to no response and glanced through more of the notes, realizing he had indeed likely lost his mind.

There were stacks of black-and-white printouts of cubes within cubes, of a spiral over squares I recognized as the golden ratio, and there were notes with numbers crossed out with only the number nine circled at the bottom surrounded by an underlined 90°. Images of three-by-three grids and unfolded cubes were crossed out as if proven incorrect with thick, black marker. Other printouts were of the nine worlds of Norse mythology, of biblical passages of the movement of god and Dante's nine circles of hell. There were wiki pages on Egyptian history and a group of gods named "Ennead," as well as random pages from numerology. Pages that I completely refused to believe the Brian I knew would even humor reading, let alone print out. If it wasn't for his tall, looping cursive I used to tease him about, I would've assume this the work of someone else entirely.

I called out loudly once more before noticing the blueprints, plans for a rectangle that was nearly a square, comprised of nine perfect squares of varying sizes. I remembered from algebra many years ago and the term, stuck on the precipice of my mind, that finally tumbled forth: a perfect rectangle. "2, 5, 7, 9, 16, 25, 28, 33, 36" marked the boxes within the box on diagram, and underneath was a blueprint scaled up to 138 feet by 122 feet, and I realized these numbers might correspond to the massive structure before me. "Brian?" I shouted at the large building within the walls of the barn.

I approached the strange construction, opening the door of the entrance to peek inside. Vertical beams of cedar stretched between the wooden floor and tall ceiling of the empty room. There was one door was on the wall to the right. I entered the room that seemed to be about fifty square feet and felt a cold chill on my skin, confused by how an additional wall of insulation from the winter air could cause the temperature to drop.

"Brian, are you in here?" I called loudly, my voice echoing flatly off of the wooden walls. I heard a steady humming once inside that reminded me of a fan, but the source seemed to be coming from further within the structure. I continued on, trying to fight off the uneasy feeling welling in my stomach.

I walked further to the door's knob, turned it slowly, and pushed it open. I was assaulted by a horrible stench that filled the darkness. I removed my phone and switched on the light before stepping in, confused at the feeling of pressure building like growing marbles inside of my ears. I stopped in my tracks, staring at the decaying body on the floor, where white bone peeked through the blotchy, necrotic flesh that was once a face.

"Oh no, no, no, Brian!" I called out, walking slowly to the side of the body, covering my nose with my jacket sleeve and noticing the matching color. He was wearing the same jacket, his stained with the noxious fluids of putrefaction. I stared for a few moments at the decaying corpse and realized every single article of clothing—his jeans, his tan work boots, and even his tousled hair on papery skin—was the same as my own.

I kneeled by the putrid body and picked up the wallet by his side, and it was my wallet, the one Brian had sent me a photo of. Every detail was undeniably the same, even the wrinkled $20 bills with folds in the same places, marked with identical serial numbers. My license and the scuff marks on my credit cards were identical in every way: every nick, scratch, and crease. I cringed as I stared into the horrible, lipless scream of a mouth, able to make out the fillings in the teeth that matched my very own. I shivered as horror and madness dripped from my lizard brain when the feeling of immediate danger forced me to my shaky legs and screamed at me to leave.

I ran back to the door I'd entered from, half expecting it to be locked and beyond relieved it wasn't. I spilled back into the first chamber, claustrophobia gripping my throat as I ran to the exit and pushed the door open in confusion as any sense of relief was replaced by dread. The door opened to an adjacent room of identical structure, wooden in entirety with only a door to the left and the one behind me I'd entered from.

I ran to the other door, opening it fast and wheezing with hyperventilation from my peaking confusion, I was in another identical room. It was impossible. The rooms could not have been shifted or rearranged; the doors were framed and securely constructed in place.

Even if somehow that had been the case, the entrance I'd come in through was less than two meters from the wall of the barn itself.

I paced back and forth, telling myself it was a dream, almost laughing because this simply wasn't possible. I tossed some pocket change onto the pine floor. I continued to the next door, noticing for the first time the springs on the hinges that closed them automatically. I opened the door to find an identical room yet again and paused as my brain tried to understand the structure I was in but to no avail. I backtracked to the previous room to find the change missing, and I laughed loudly as madness dissolved the rationale that had been encoded for decades into my brain.

I pounded on the sturdy pine walls with my fist, lit by the light of the phone in my other hand, and I saw that the signal was present but I was unable to make a call. I then noticed the time: 9:12 a.m. I wondered how I could have been in this strange structure for over half a day in what felt like twenty minutes. The shock and confusion of how I'd become trapped slipped slowly away as I peered up to the corner of the phone's screen, processing the date. December 11th, 2017, was glowing in a thin white font, not January 20th, 2018, the day I drove here. It wasn't until I opened Facebook and read Brian's last post that unease wrenched my stomach.

"Seeing an old friend today," I read above a now-clear photo of my collapsed body as I heard the closing of a door from another room.

GOD ISN'T DEAD, HE WAS JUST SLEEPING

A rich couple in Vermont discovered it, according to the reports I'd read. They had started construction on a new home on property they'd purchased in the Finger Lakes, a getaway that got away once the crew first found the peculiarity in the frozen soil. They took photos and supplied them to my company, which handled larger drilling jobs and very rarely worked for individuals. The photos showed an odd, translucent wall of what appeared to be some kind of mineral formation that was over three meters long and slightly curved. It was like nothing I'd seen, but nothing compared to what I was going to, either.

The six of us drove down, and I had the luck of taking the LoDril LM60, a beast of machinery but a nightmare to drive long distances. Despite infuriated drivers honking and screaming obscenities, I finally made it up the winding road to the construction site. It was exposed, a monolith of foggy white like a short wall. We began digging around it, assessing the size in order to pull it with the help of a crane, but we hit something else just a meter down that was even more confusing. It was a large rounded area of what appeared to be an enormous stump at first, but the team kept hauling dirt until a mound the size of a large room was unearthed. We all stared in disbelief at the ridges on the pink form and began to realize the lines weren't the age rings of an ancient tree at all, but the swirling, patterned grooves of a fingerprint.

Our team grew as more men and larger machines were driven in, and for weeks the digging continued. The fingertip did actually descend downward to a massive finger, buried for untold millennia. It was weeks before the entire hand was revealed, roughly the size of a two-story building, and the project continued as the enormous arm was eventually dug out. When the head had been unearthed, the crew began acting nervous and frantic; it took up much of an entire city block. The religious members soon quit, followed by the superstitious, and as new help was recruited, pay rates jumped. Everyone refused to dig once the eyes opened, however, and that leads us to today.

We retreated the equipment as far as we could before panic set in when the rumble of the quaking earth tossed us to the ground as the buried entity crawled out of the ancient resting place. We watched from a nearby hill through uncontrollable tears at the titan emerged from his tomb. The horrible look in the mammoth's bulging, insane eyes made me sick, and I trembled as the gargantuan being was birthed from the ground after uncountable years of stasis. A humongous arm swept slowly over, plucking a praying worker up between the tips of fingernails and tossed him into his massive, open mouth. We knew we had messed up terribly and irreversibly, but the only thing we could do then was watch.

MY DOG IS GAY

People have yelled on dozens of occasions that my dog is gay as they confront me in the dog park. My Lab is often found straddling the pets of very annoyed dog owners, who seem to have issues regarding their own sexuality. Despite leashing him immediately, I've gotten shouted at, degraded, and demeaned to the point I want to hit these guys. Their threatened machismo always spills out with a stream of insults, homophobic slurs, and red-faced rage. I stand there as their furious spit flecks my glasses, and I bite my tongue. This is often my life at the dog park, as it was yesterday.

My sweet golden Lab was gallivanting about, playing with, then humping on every god-fearing man's dog when he began dominating a Mastiff. They are massive breeds, as was this one, with floppy jowls and an intimidating stance not unlike its accompanying human. The owner was tall, three hundred forty pounds maybe, with a graying beard and a tattooed trucker's look. He grabbed my shirt from my chest in a balled fist and breathed the cavity-assisted stench of rotten breath in my face as he declared, "Get your faggot dog the fuck away from mine if you want to see tomorrow."

I hate that word, I'm straight yet oh-so-single that you might think it makes no difference, but something about the hateful, threatening tone of this asshole really set me off. I smiled in his angry face, pulled Tucker by his leash, and retreated with him back to my car to decompress. I saw that asshole bring his massive, scary dog into an oversized gas guzzler and rev his engine like his small dick needed some noise to hide behind. I followed that piece of living shit back to his copy-paste, gauche suburban house.

I know, I sound like a creep, a stalker and the likes, and I deserve that. Know, however, my actions were a show. It was just a game I was playing to justify living on this planet with people who act like that. A fantasy before I drove away like the passive man I truly am.

It was an act of following, envisioning action, and then leaving that I was engaged in, until I saw the eyes in the slit of his basement window.

I know that at some point you have felt pure, seething terror.

Whether it was a bad trip, a threatening ex, or an actual dance with death, you may have felt that raw, unfiltered fear. There is something about the eyes that lets loose in those moments, when the mask of civility and humanity dissipates into the ether as it is unleashed. A stallion of seething nightmare pounds into your lizard brain, destroying any chance of composure and creating a wide stare that is unmistakable as they scream out in need of help. That is the look I saw in those eyes.

I waited, parked on his street, until he hopped out of his massive truck with his intimidating dog. I waited until he unlocked the front door of his oversized, ticky-tacky home. I waited until night fully fell, and I fetched a boxcutter from my glove box and a tire iron from the back of my car and crept around to the back, easily slipping in the bathroom window, which was unlocked. I gripped my tire iron tight and solid snaked my way into the porcelain, spotless bathroom. I eased that door open silently and observed the monster watching videos of children on his computer, his back to me. I saw the opening to the stairwell and descended in absolute silence.

I came upon a door, which was locked with an absurd series of deadbolts, and entered. I saw the child, bound and gagged near the window, the blood on the floor and the tools on the table. Metal, rusty tools, and other items I will not mention. Things that built up a loathing I was previously unable to process. I pressed my finger to my lips, and the child understood. I removed my boxcutter and severed the rope that was so tightly bound on their bloodied wrist. I led them slowly up the stairs and to the bathroom. It was easy for them to crawl outside to freedom. It wasn't at all easy for the owner of that home.

That dog did nothing wrong, and I felt bad enough my Tucker had humiliated him at the park. It was him or me, however, as he charged into that bathroom after hearing the kid escape, baring those massive teeth. The dog clenched down onto my forearm, the excruciating pain burning before I knocked the drooling hound out with a swing of the tire iron. That hefty man watching children on his computer came next, but he wasn't getting off with sleep. He began by screaming insults and hurling fists, but soon he was spraying blood and flinging strips of flesh from his neck and jaw. His eyeball spilled out like a poached egg from a gory hole in his flayed, dripping face as I went to work. He screamed to the point I thought his vocal cords would explode before he finally went silent from the boxcutter's sculpting.

I'm not posting any details about the location, the child, or the scum that needed removal for obvious reasons. I will, however, post my dog's details so you can praise him when you see him. According to a few guys at the dog park, my dog is gay, as if that's somehow a negative trait in their shallow minds. His name is Tucker, and he's a sweet Lab that annoys the hell out of dogs and humans all over town. He isn't the smartest, and he shits in the house on occasion, but I love him, and last night he saved a child's life.

I CONFRONTED THE PEEPING CREEP IN MY BUILDING

Cindy's shout from the bathroom jolted me awake, each word crisp and angry. "Someone's watching me shower!" Cindy had a way of amplifying her voice when upset, as I'd learned through my own past mistakes and poorly timed jokes. I turned my head to the door with some effort and spoke.

"You sure?" I asked groggily, still half asleep.

"Yes, I even see a goddamned telescope! I hate this city and the filthy pervs here," she yelled, a quaver in her tone warning of an onset of tears.

"Coming, babe," I said in a raspy voice before clearing my throat, and I braced my eyes for the bright light of the hallway and bathroom. As I stood, my gaze lingered on the red LED clock that taunted me with the numbers 1:52 a.m. I dragged my bare feet on the wooden stretch over to the bathroom and joined my girlfriend, who wore a nightgown and a scowl. I began rubbing her shoulders as if to mend the problem as she spoke.

"There, look," Cindy said, pointing a fingernail out the window to the building on the other end of the courtyard. "He lives in our damned building, probably been rubbing them out daily when I shower, oh god!" Cindy was rattled, a rarity from the strong woman who'd found me when I had truly needed her. I peered at the silhouetted form through squinted eyes that continued to adjust from the bathroom's brightness, but I could make out the staring man and the gleaming light reflecting off a lens. Sure enough, someone was peeping in.

"I'll take care of it tomorrow, honey," I promised before kissing her cheek and switching off the light. He still stared in, unfazed. The audacity of this pervert really got under my skin. Cindy had dealt with harassment before, a slender woman who would punch a nose bloody when confronted, but she was understandably vulnerable being watched in the confines of our apartment. "I'll make him stop, you have my word. Nobody messes with my gal." I gave her a smile, and she flipped the bird to the window before we finally headed back to the bedroom to sleep.

A nightmare plagued my dreams, surely inspired by the creep staring in, and I was first to the shower after waking early. I brought in a hand towel and tape to block the small window, but I again saw that creep staring in at me, his body shaking and hunched as if pleasuring himself. I was beyond disgusted, this guy was shameless, and I made sure to count the number of windows to locate his apartment. I flipped the asshole off and proceeded to tape up the towel before my routine, and when Cindy's frazzled, red hair popped into the bathroom, a wry look accompanied a "really?"

"I'll get a curtain after work, and more importantly, I'm confronting him tonight. Just use this in the meantime," I suggested.

"You mean he's still looking in?" I looked up again, seeing him shift in his chair, staring in with that telescope pointed straight at us. I nodded, and Cindy rolled her eyes. "You better confront that piece of trash, no wimping out like you did at that New Year's party."

Ouch.

So I didn't beat up a drunk man who'd shoved past her to high five his DJ friend. She knew how to salt my wounds, but she smiled and slapped my butt before using the restroom after me. "Just talk to that asshole or I will." I had every intention of talking to him, and by talk I meant confront with a closed fist if it came to that. I was livid.

Work flew by with some annoyances, and it became clear my compromised privacy was making me very irritable. When I finally left for the day and picked up a curtain, I made a list of things to say to make sure the pervert never even looked out his window again. I was riled up when I got home, but when I lifted the towel to see the fidgeting silhouette staring in once more, I saw red. Not five minutes home, I was out the door and climbing the stairs one extra floor and found myself rounding the building's corners to stand at the door I knew was his. I heard some hissing sound from inside that sounded like a running tap, and I knocked loud and clear five times to make sure he heard.

"I know you're in there. I just saw you staring into my bathroom window," I stated loudly and waited a good ten seconds before knocking harder. The door eased open a crack from my knocking, and I gritted my teeth before I let my foot "accidentally" ease the door open a bit more. Through a cluttered living room stocked with nature books and travel guides, I could see him seated in his bedroom while that hiss of a running tap grew louder. I stared in from the hallway at the older, naked man in the next room, jiggling in his chair and holding a long instrument to the window.

I stepped in, further calling out to him, knowing I was entering a stranger's apartment, but guided by my need to understand how every part of this guy—arms, legs, face and chest—seemed to be vibrating unnaturally. He looked to be having a seizure, but every square inch of him moved at a different rate. I stepped into the space as unease sent shivers down my spine. When I was finally close enough to see him clearly, my mind was screaming that something was very wrong.

The man sitting in the chair held a scoped rifle; the scope was what had appeared to be a telescope pointed at our window. The stock rested on his windowsill and extended up to the barrel resting in his mouth in a suicide, clear by a red splatter flecking the ceiling and walls behind him. What was far more concerning was the source of the sound and why he was moving. His skin rippled like thin cloth from thousands of large insects that crawled from his nose to his mouth, his ears to that exit wound, causing him to jiggle and bob but remain upright. The man had clearly killed himself, and his body was completely overtaken, stripped of meat and his skin plump and writhing from the insects inside. Perhaps the strangest thing of all was how there was barely any odor, as if he'd just died.

My eyes widened in disbelief as I observed a group of the insects that resembled large earwigs wriggling down his carpet quickly in my direction, emanating that hissing sound. I let out a guttural yell and quickly backed out his door, pulling it shut before backtracking into the hallway. I began to wonder how those bugs could arrive so quickly and in such great numbers to a corpse who had so recently died, and then a terrifying thought brewed in the corners of my mind. I raced down the carpet to the stairs, considering the awful possibility that he shot himself after they arrived.

I booked a hotel and told Cindy to come to the address straight from work before I called the police to report the incident. I told the dispatcher something was very wrong and they should evacuate the building immediately, explaining the aggressive bugs, but they sounded determined to check it out themselves. Only Cindy seemed to believe me, tearful and equally freaked out as we soberly checked into the hotel.

I sit on the edge of the hotel bed shivering, unable to shake the sight of that man's body, swarming like a full fishing net and upright even in death. Cindy cleans up in the bathroom after a fit of tears, my own eyes puffy from the same act. The steady hiss of the faucet has been going for far too long now, but I can't bear to call to Cindy through the door. I can't say a word as I'm terrified to confirm what my anguished mind already suspects, that the bathroom faucet is off.

15 MINUTES IS NOT ENOUGH

Everyone seeps the same drivel about my ship having sailed, my fifteen minutes being up, my dream realized. I hear the snickers and see the side-eyed glances that accompany a giggling grin. I see the piranha tabloids documenting my fall from grace, catching me mid-chew when I dine. Those vultures watch and wait eagerly for my body to drop so they can feed on my carrion. Oh, I am going to feed them. I'm going to make them eat their garbage words, one putrid sliver at a time.

I hit LA in the seventies with my muscles, machismo, and mustached smile. I don't kiss and tell, so I won't describe my romantic conquests; just know many women forgot their significant other existed when I walked brazenly into a room. I had the cars. I had the women. I had everything. I would fly first class to shoot in New Zealand or Austria in dramas you revere as classics. Films that decorate your collection and are the standard by which you judge. My third wife used to say, "You invented the burly sex symbol," and she meant it, bless her maggot-infested heart. She was the first costar and the first to learn my fifteen minutes are far from up.

Media is always evolving, and I've come to terms with that. My first film used beautiful 35mm in its grainy, artful glory. Later, video and videotapes were the rage, and when my films went straight to DVD, I knew that big, bright spotlight was shifting. It drifted slowly but surely to those younger, fresher stars and starlets who didn't rise from the dirt as I had. I saw their shiny, fresh bodies and perfect white smiles. My reflection taunts me with the sag of wrinkled skin and receding gray hair. It torments and mocks, but I know how to get that spotlight back.

I'm working on my greatest role even now, my fingers still stained red with congealed blood.

I started with the vile paparazzi. They'd sneak those hideous shots of me from the bushes at first but were easily persuaded inside with a tall glass of lemonade and liberty to take photos. Once the lemonade hits, their body becomes the player in my magnum opus. The camera rests on the tripod, focusing on their draped form as I, the star, step into frame. Their sallow skin splits easy with a razor as I strip gripping veins and clingy muscle from bone. I make a dramatic use of scenery by ramming the chair leg into those food-flecked teeth, cracking the jaw as it descends.

I hear the snide whispers and read the insulting comments on the message boards. I may not have the wealth I once had, but I can easily muster the funds to pay the Romanian computer whiz who responded to my ad. He identifies the information of the transgressing actors-to-be in the form of lists. His accuracy is astounding, dropping a Google Map pin and a clear photo to hunt them like rats. I travel to them daily now, dressing as a UPS worker delivering a package only I will open. A package containing a camera, a tripod, and a set of razors eager to assist my performance.

I flay flesh in jiggling chunks from faces, rip wobbling fat from muscle, and scrape blood-slicked tendons from glistening bone. I film it all, each lip slivered off, each bone snapped and shattered, with my award-winning acting emphasizing each gouge, rip, and tear. I destroy the competition, literally, when I hunt the new names of rising stars that pop up on those billboards.

I see the endless exposure given to the killers in the news.

Everyone knows Manson and Bundy, Zodiac, and now DeAngelo.

Adapting was as easy as trading in VHS for DVDs and then MP4s. I merely saw where the spotlight drifted and swerved to stay in it. My fifteen minutes will stretch out to stain history, eternal and delicious as cancer.

I'm hunting down extras, and you may unwittingly apply when posting a comment where my hacker forages. My greatest film is still in production, but when it debuts, you will forever remember my name.

THE OLDEST BIBLE HAS BEEN TRANSLATED

When the book was discovered in nearly perfect condition, the press went wild. They had found what predated the oldest known bible, complete and in miraculous shape, by nearly three thousand years. A set of strikingly familiar stories were entombed in the unnaturally well-preserved and carbon-dated, ancient holy book. Each of the stories was far darker than any version that had been remodeled to suit the morals by which societies have since held. It was shorter as well at four hundred forty-four pages, and as the book's translation began and excerpts made their way into the news, we soon discovered why.

It began with God creating the universe in six days, choosing not to take a seventh to rest. God was described in unsettling detail, however, his insectile claws and writhing tentacles shaping objects while fiendish jaws laughed during the manic creation. Other similarities arose as well, but they grew stranger as each section was translated. After God ripped out Adam and Eve's ribs, licking their blood up, he demanded all firstborn be sacrificed as blood offerings.

Only the second child and on could live. The story of Noah and the flood was in there, too, but the animals were used for heinous acts in order to create abominations for his amusement.

God was often described as cackling his many fanged mouths in joy at the suffering of mankind and licking blistered lips during forced acts of brutality. In fact, it became clear when passages were referenced and covered less frequently by the press that something absolutely hideous had been unearthed. It became clear why anyone would try and clean up the graphic stories. The Ten Commandments were missing entirely, and the Seven Deadly Sins were listed, though as daily atonement to be spared for engaging in when God finally returned.

Translators puzzled and explored other possible interpretations, but it soon became clear that this version seemed to also prophesize accurate future events, disasters, and wars, such as praise for the atrocities of a world-involved war and many other notable massacres.

The bible referenced world powers rising and building blocks being split to create great weapons, scarily similar to the atom bomb.

Religious wars and conflicts were predicted, even the falling of a metropolis's towers, listing 2,996 dead as on 9/11.

As the last of the two hundred thousand words were being translated, the entire world was reading and listening along in growing trepidation.

The last few pages described the billions to be stripped of skin to rot in the red sun and be pecked of their meat upon the god's catastrophic return. The very last page explained that the sky would bleed during his arrival, commencing shortly after the book's own self-referenced translation, when all would scramble to kill their firstborn. I read as the last word of the translation finished the feed, then turned in horror as the night's sky glowed crimson, before the screams from out the window began.

HELL IS IN COLUMBIA, SOUTH DAKOTA

I live on the outskirts of Columbia, South Dakota, and in case you've never been, here's a brief tour:

Pros:

- Beautiful, picturesque sunsets
- Ample room for pets to run about
- Aberdeen is close by, and they have some fun establishments
- Peace, quiet, and privacy

Cons:

- Boredom. There is not a lot to do here aside from feeling like you're missing out
- The economy isn't exactly booming
- The meth heads, they aren't abundant but they are here
- Peace, quiet, and privacy

I have two dogs, a cat, and a horse. Moxie's a lab-pit mix with an addiction to licking your hand and begging. Carl is a boxer mutt, and his superpower is farts that traumatize you. Penelope, my cat, has a fluffy, white coat and emerald eyes that might allure you, but she will scratch your hand like there's catnip inside; don't try to pet her. Simon is my horse, a handsome, chestnut friend who listens to my woes and minds his own. They are my family, and I love them dearly and equally, so when I woke up today, my heart fluttered in my chest with worry at a high-pitched sound. The animals were screaming.

My blood ran cold. My beloved pups were making a sound I had never heard, belting out an anguished cry I thought only humans were capable of. I called their names and ran to find them facing the front door, not howling, not barking, but screaming. I began petting their backs and confirming their well-being, and they looked completely unharmed. Carl's eyes were filled with fear, and he turned to me and ceased that awful sound when I arrived at his side. Moxie stopped as well, then panted and whimpered at something on the other side of the door. It was surreal and haunting; I half expected the devil himself to knock any second from their behavior.

I peeped out the window, seeing nothing but my cat on the lawn. I scooped some clattering dry food into their bowls before hearing more screaming from outside the house. I grabbed a flannel shirt from the rack and swung open the door to hear a high-pitched scream from the lawn. Penelope, my cat, was making that terrible scream, facing me but staring at the grass near the solitary crabapple tree. I called her name, and she looked up at me with a startled expression before silencing her strange cries and bounding off to the barn for Simon's protection. What in God's name were they alarmed by? I'd never heard those sounds from them, or any other animal for that matter, in my entire life. I walked to the grass near the tree that Penelope had been staring at and saw a small black hole in the lawn.

I peered in, wondering if it was an old well or an exposed septic tank from the previous owner. It surely wasn't there the last time I'd mowed the lawn, back when Charlene was living with me. To be honest, I let the lawn, and myself, go unattended for the past year. I looked into the tortilla-sized hole, seeing nothing but blackness. I was dressed in boxers and a flannel, not that my nearest neighbor could see me from here, but I wanted to get dressed and get my flashlight before investigating further. That's all I would've asked, and I would've been at terms with the injustice the fates bestowed upon me. I would've not cursed them as much once the ground collapsed under my weight, and my stomach met my throat as I dropped in a free-fall into the pit. I could count the seconds as I fell into the opening darkness, until I hit the cold, hard ground with a slap.

I yelled out in pain as my ribs bent from my body's weight and my elbow cracked on the firm, stone floor in that pit. My yells echoed in the vast, underground chamber as I listed every expletive in my vocabulary and squeezed my arm near the stinging elbow. I was in intense pain after having fallen what must've been forty feet, and there was likely a hairline fracture in the bone. I looked up at the small hole I'd fallen through, amazed at how far away it was. I once again yelled the list of curses I knew as I rose to my feet on the smooth floor of the hidden cavern I was clearly trapped inside of.

I tried in vain to climb the jagged ridges that curved inward like the walls of a dome up to the opening, but the fact that the pit grew wider near the base made it impossible. I limped over on a sore leg to the stone walls of the large chamber, noticing the unmistakable stench of death that the animals surely noticed far before I had. It was a distraction from the pain, but worrisome to say the least. *How many animals have fallen in here and died?* I wondered. My dread blended with the subterranean air, cold and tinged with death, to shiver my exposed skin. I wished I had jeans or even shoes on. I wished I had a signal on my cell to call someone. I wished my nearest neighbor was a friend who would eventually come by and hear my screams. I wished Moxie or Carl were at my side as I ran my fingers on the cold, dark stone of the walls that seemed symmetrical and almost decorated with texture.

My eyes slowly adjusted to the vast chamber, and I began to make out the shapes on obsidian walls and along a floor that seemed far too smooth to be nature's work. My eyes adjusted to see an arcing, jagged passage to my left. Crystalline formations of an onyx hue ornamented the opening and beckoned me to investigate. I then saw the bones of animals before noticing the larger skulls and unmistakable, crumbled human limbs. I began to see the tibiae, fibulae, and ribs, stripped completely of any remnant of flesh. I saw a hammered tin container from what must have been a century ago and opened it up to find shards of flint, some wax, pine tar, and a metal *C*; it was a flint and steel kit from a different time.

I hammered down on the flint with the metal for what must have been an hour, screaming to that hole above for help till my throat was scratchy and raw. I came to terms with the fact that nobody could hear me, but I eventually sparked that rope into fire and dipped it in the melting wax to sustain the flame. My relief at getting it lit was quickly replaced with dread as I gazed in slack-jawed wonder at the impossibly perfect shape of a massive dome the orange flame had lit up.

There were dozens of human and animal remains, and what looked like rat holes where the walls met the floor. The holes looked unnaturally smooth like the floor, curving softly inward as if carved by a sculptor. Empty tins that likely once held food from another century were scattered about, as well as a few books that crumbled like ash from my touch. Black graffiti, mostly illegible, covered the dark gray walls that curved up to that taunting, impossible-to-reach hole. The writing on the walls was archaic, and I could only make out one passage in English that seemed to be written by fingers.

"I pray th're a heaven, I did see hell."

I then realized the words, each and every one of the characters and what looked like glyphs, were written in blood. I found a barely intact book on the smooth ground, mottled with foxing, and realized it was a very old bible. I flipped to the date and read with a frown; it was printed 1662. I dropped the book with the growing realization I might not ever get out of this place, my remains possibly undiscovered for hundreds of years like the skeletons around me.

I held the lit rope's flickering orange flame up to the chamber's only exit, that tall archway, and walked through to see a massive descending staircase with carved, onyx steps that lowered in a winding descent. The stairwell walls were spotted with holes the size of tea saucers that decorated it in a peculiar pattern. I slowly approached one, holding out the flame in my hand to illuminate it, and quickly covered my mouth at the sight of what squirmed inside.

Skin-colored caterpillars, with small human heads and tiny human arms in place of their many legs, crawled hypnotically throughout the hole. Dozens of the horrible forms climbed the walls and dangled from the top by sticky, tiny-fingered hands. I nearly giggled as madness poked a fingernail into my brain as I stared into the tiny faces that smiled menacingly at me. Soulless, black eyes rested above thin quills of razor-sharp teeth, visible through sickening smiles as the oddities crawled and clambered over each other.

I shook my head and looked back to the chamber I'd come from in order to retreat but then saw the newly huddled forms peering down at me from that top stair. They must have crawled from the holes I'd seen lining the walls, flesh-colored, hairless rats hunched on scrambling, tiny hands with malevolent smiles fixed on human faces. I jerked my bare foot as I felt tiny hands claw at, and then I ran. I ran down the spiral staircase and into the unknown darkness, realizing there had to be another way out further inside the horrible and impossible place. A place that I began to realize, as the writing on the wall resonated, was hell itself.

FLIGHT 347 CAME BACK

I watched the somber faces of families, huddled and sniffling as they waited eagerly for news about their loved ones. It was a standard, daily flight from Detroit to LGA in New York, but the storm had caused delays. As the reports came in from air traffic control that the flight crew was not responding, the rumors spread throughout the airport, and before long, the situation unfolded into panic as wailing mothers, sobbing fiancées, and praying grandmothers filled the gate with a dismal chill. My eyes watered and nose streamed as well with the rumors of a problem; my sister Sam was on board the plane.

Each passing hour, it became more apparent a tragedy was unfolding. I offered some tissues to a whimpering mother who wouldn't stop saying "my baby" over and over again. As the hours ticked slowly by, the realization we were dealing with a devastating loss of lives became realer and more upsetting. Families began to trickle out to find hotels for the evening. As the evening sank into the full of night, more and more left, but I waited for my sister, eventually falling asleep on the vinyl seating of the gate's waiting area.

The next day, I awoke to a mess of people demanding answers, and they had none. When the pilots had been in contact, nothing out of the ordinary was mentioned, and no flights had gone down anywhere along the flight path. "You are just hiding the truth from us to save your ass!" screamed an irate, balding man awaiting the arrival of his wife and daughters. The mob grew angry, but it soon became clear the uniformed woman behind the counter knew nothing we didn't already.

The patient woman shared each communication, as did the customer service managers, and we had no option but to wait for news. By the end of the day, most families had stumbled out of the airport defeated, realizing their loved ones were likely dead in a crash.

I scoured the news feeds constantly, refreshing for any development the first few days. There was nothing of note aside for news of the missing plane with every detail we already knew, and soon the media began covering the plane's disappearance as a disaster, declaring it the largest missing commercial plane since Flight 370. It became clear my sister was dead, and I began drinking a bit more and lashing out at my friends and coworkers, unable to truly process my grief. Sam had been my best friend my entire life, a tomboy rocker with a comedian's wit and a heart of gold. It all felt so unfair, yet still I tried to come to terms with her loss.

I began talking to my parents in Michigan daily, reliving memories of childhood, graduation, and holiday blunders. After a week of talking with my parents on the phone, they began discussing funeral arrangements, and reality slapped me hard once more. I was ready to accept it this time, however, and agreed to fly back home to help them with the planning.

I booked a ticket online and cabbed to LaGuardia after work that Friday, a bit uneasy about flying but far more concerned with having to say goodbye to my sister via an empty grave. When I arrived at the airport and saw news vans parked outside, I pushed through and began to overhear earfuls of gossip and rumors that floated about in growing confusion as I pieced the news together about what the commotion was about. Flight 347 had returned.

I listened to the gray-haired man with rolled sleeves yell to the gathered crowd as he explained everything he knew. The plane just popped up on the radar and was cleared to land. He said no known damage had occurred, and as far as he knew, everyone was likely on board and accounted for. I listened in disbelief; there was no way that flight would have enough fuel to stay aloft for such an extensive period of time. And what had it possibly been doing, circling for a week straight? Mostly, however, I was overwhelmed with the possibility that Sam was actually alive.

My information came in pieces, and soon the families I had waited alongside that first, dreadful night showed up, eager to be reunited with their loved ones. I saw familiar, tear-streaked faces and heard many use the words "miracle," "impossible," and "guardian angel." I smiled and thought of there being some kind of higher power that somehow brought our families back, and soon we received news that the missing Flight 347 was to be deboarded. The crowd erupted in celebratory cheers.

I canceled my flight and excitedly relayed the news as it occurred to my parents, who cried with joy at the unexpected miracle. I accepted a plastic cup of wine from a mother I'd shared tissues with that first harrowing night. It felt surreal, almost like a dream, and in reality I knew it was like a dream; these things simply don't happen.

People simply don't come back from a week missing from their flight pattern. Still, I cheered and hugged those eager to see our beloved missing families. We clapped and cried as the plane arrived without a hitch and waited by the doors as the passenger boarding bridge was brought out. The first of the arrival crew headed to greet them, and excitement built, but then we heard a scream.

Minutes slowed as we waited until finally, the staggering employee, holding herself up with the wall, came into view. She was pale and wide-eyed, a thousand-yard stare frozen on her freckled, previously smiling face. A help desk employee tried to assist her, but she seemed vacant and detached, and soon a security officer joined the side of the help desk employee as they headed into the skyway to the plane that came back.

After a few long minutes, they too returned, pale, sweaty, uniforms stained with fresh vomit. The woman from the desk was rocking and shaking her head and soon began scratching her eyes until the security officer physically restrained her arms to prevent her from blinding herself. We all stood by and gawked with growing concern.

When the passengers finally began to emerge from the skyway, screaming and crying echoed through the gate as my eyes fought to adjust to what I was looking at exactly.

They came back, every passenger on that flight, and they all came back wrong. My mind tried to understand the sickening forms of legs that folded too many times and hands that festered with rot and decay. Malformed limbs dragged misplaced bones and entrails, none of which belonged where they now resided, streaking the carpet black as those terrifying figures emerged. The disturbing collages that once were humans now spilled into that gate, staining the minds of each one of us as sanity teetered and crashed into crumbs at the horrors of what had become of them.

I bit my finger until I bled, stumbling backward as one by one, they approached, each somehow more ghastly than the last. I collapsed to the carpeted floor when I saw that hideous thing I knew was once Sam from her clothes drag its torso, now more of a clumped, bone-filled mess behind that warped, nightmarish head that howled a sickening moan. There was only one collective thought all the waiting family members shared now that Flight 347 came back, and it was that we all wished more than anything that it had not.

EVERY DAY I DIE

Every day I live a life just like you perhaps might. I wake up and eat breakfast, go to work, then eat lunch, finish work, and eat dinner. I might enjoy drinks or a movie out, but at some point, I crawl into bed, and I eventually sleep. The varied details are not relevant to my predicament; my day is generally like many other days in many other lives. What differs is that every time I drift off to sleep, I immediately awaken.

I used to think they were elaborate dreams. I remember being a child, discussing dreams with friends, and witnessing their confusion when I asked, "Who were you last night?" Blank stares were followed by their continued conversation of nightmares, monsters, flying a jet plane, or exploring magical worlds. It sounded fun and incredible, and I envied them. My dreams, every one of them, were reliving the final moments of a stranger before their life was extinguished.

I'd awaken in a hospital bed, my skin spotted and wrinkled, unfamiliar family members at my side and tubes shoved deep in my nostrils. The family would call me Barbara or Janice or Nana, tears streaming down their faces as they told me they loved me and heaven awaited. I'd ask where I was and who they were. I'd explain my name was Michael and I was eight, and they'd break down into fits of tears and mumble words I'd first hear then. Words like dementia, Alzheimer's, and Huntington's disease. They'd weep and whimper as I faded away, and then I'd wake up drenched in sweat, back in my bed and back in my young body.

Other days I fell asleep and woke in automotive plants or car repair shops. Some large, tanned men with oil-stained overalls would shout a name repeatedly before I realized they were speaking to me.

Angry faces confronted me, accusing me of drinking on the job, threatening my termination, and I'd be ordered to get back under a suspended Chevy or remove the loose, steel part clogging a conveyor belt. Soon after, a four-ton car would drop down, crushing my chest with an excruciating crack, or my uniform's sleeve would catch in the belt as it was accidentally turned on, yanking me inward to be mangled with white-hot pain as I screamed. Panicked shouting would fill the space as I bled to death, and I'd then wake up, damp and feverish in my bed once again.

I talked to my parents, and they explained dreams were simply that. They were the mind's playground of coping mechanisms, and maybe I should focus on figuring out what I wanted to do with my life rather than fixating on death, but I couldn't control it. Every night I dreaded falling asleep. I'd even sneak into my parents' coffee beans and chew them to stay awake, but eventually, even if a day later, it would happen all over again.

I'd be floating in warm fluid with fleshy walls, my fingers tiny and see-through. I breathed underwater somehow, by some tube from my belly, and I smelled what my mother smelled outside. I felt shivers as she grew distressed, and I felt the cord around my neck, strangling me as my blood flow stopped until I awoke.

I'd be surrounded by other children, playing in the sand while strange music played, wearing a long, white shirt that extended to my shoes. The kids spoke a language I didn't understand, and when I asked them what they were saying, I received peculiar looks. An explosion deafened me as clouds of dust and red spray burst out, and fragments of bodies littered the ground as screams wailed. I looked to my feet, but they were gone, only red flesh spilling from my chest as I faded away to wake in my bed, once again in the warm beams of the sun.

This happened every single night; a new death awaited me, and each day I remembered details of these dreams that I couldn't have possibly known. I'd wander into the living room as my parents watched the news, and I'd see familiar adult faces in the background of a drone strike. I'd peek at my father's paper and see obituaries of people whose name I had been called by tearful relatives on my deathbed. I'd remember urgent words and tearful goodbyes in Lao, Urdu, German, and Japanese. I could recall particular words and details, and when I looked them up later to confirm them, I began to understand these dreams were real.

By the time I was a teenager, I began attempting to intervene with fate by avoiding death. They mostly seemed inevitable, like a dead fall from miles up, wind rippling my skin as I skydived with a defective shoot. I'd try and yank the cord, try to slow my descent to that surreal, expanding Earth below, but nothing worked as I slowly plunged to finally slam down on solid ground with an agonizing crunch.

Another day, I was alone in an apartment, seeing my naked female body in the shower, wet from the beating faucet, and I slipped out as quickly as possible. I searched for a bed to hide under, but a large, abusive ex still yanked me out by my bruising arm. I smelled the whiskey on his breath as he began spewing horrible curses and demeaning insults before pressing that cold steel to my temple, waking me with a ringing gunshot.

I tried screaming *run* to those near me as I walked down a tile hall surrounded by lockers. The students stared and sneered at my outburst, but a kid with the rifle burst through those doors nonetheless, mowing them down just before my chest thumped hard, and I crumbled to the floor to fade out. I'd read a survivor's account the next day, that a student had tried to warn them. I knew then I wasn't simply reliving these deaths; others could hear me.

In amazement, I read through the detailed accounts from my filling in that made their presence known online. A missionary in the Amazon reported hearing an indigenous tribesman flawlessly recite a new, English-language song he couldn't have possibly known about as he lay dying from a snake bite. A news report interviewed a mother who swore her four-year-old child recited Poe's "The Raven" as fever cooked his brain. That was me in their final moments, experimenting.

I almost began to welcome this useless, unique ability, though every day I had to suffer a very real and often very painful death in someone's place. I tried to think of ways to somehow benefit from it or help others, but then two nights ago

I saw a face as I lay on the bottom of a stairwell, my wrinkled skin bruised purple around my backward-bending leg as I bled internally. A man peered from over the top of the stairwell, a man with pale skin and meticulously combed black hair who looked not at her, the senior who'd fallen, but through her pupils and into mine. I faded out from my painful injuries and awoke with panic, unable to forget those glaring eyes.

The next time I awoke, I lay in the back of an ambulance, and a plastic oxygen mask was placed over my mouth and nose. My heart throbbed painfully in my large chest, clearly struggling to function.

Before the EMT shut the door to the truck, I saw that tall man once more, closer still, standing in the crowd but staring through me with those ice-blue eyes. His narrow face hung slack and his mouth hung slightly open as he leered at me. He was watching me intently as if fully aware I did not belong there.

Yesterday, I tried not to sleep as fear grew in the back of my head. Not of the agony of suffocating in an avalanche or snapping bones a dump truck crushes accidentally, but of him. He noticed me, that I tried to change things, to affect things, and he now knows I exist. I no longer fear dying those tear-filled, agonizing deaths. I now fear only him. I fear that pale man is going to catch me and stop me from waking up at all.

MY MOTHER'S DEMENTIA IS SCARING ME

My mother was a brilliant biologist, a tenured graduate who wrote three highly praised books on entomology. She'd recently retired, and I soon learned the painful reason why. Tears trickled down her lovely, wrinkled face, and her smile wilted as she said the name of her curse the doctor had discovered: Alzheimer's. She started to lose small things at first, passwords and car keys. The disease then moved on to larger things, her cell phone, her medication, and then names. A few months ago, I moved into the house my father Jack had bought for her thirty years ago. It was my first time back in Providence since his funeral, and I knew she needed me there.

The three-story house was always too Gothic for my taste, but my mother loved the wood stove, the large rooms, and the ample attic space. I found myself at the front porch, hauling two overstuffed suitcases, committed to be by her side as she descended into the thickening fog of dementia. She greeted me at the door with searching eyes and an odd smile, clearly at a loss for my name. I reminded her as I hugged her close, telling her it was okay, that we could work on the fuzzy details. I lifted my heavy bags into what was once the guest bedroom, below my mother's room, and unpacked my laptop, toiletries, and wardrobe.

After getting settled, we shared a pleasant meal together from a nearby takeout joint. Afterward, I helped her into bed after doling out her Namzaric and Donepezil. I tried not to cry as she called me Jack and said how glad she was I was back. I was exhausted, so I retired to my bed early that night, but I woke abruptly at around two a.m. I jolted awake in the cold darkness from a thumping sound from the ceiling above me, the sound of barefoot sprinting through the rooms upstairs.

I quickly dressed and rushed up the stairs to check on my mother, and I saw her silhouetted form framed by the open bathroom door. She looked to be smiling, but it wasn't the tender smile I'd known. It was a horrible toothy grin that looked painfully wide, and as I called out, "Mom?" and switched on the light, she stopped smiling immediately, and a look of confusion twisted her face back to normal.

"Oh, Jack, it's late. Help me to bed," she requested sternly, seemingly oblivious to her actions.

"It's Michael. Sure thing, Mom," I explained and extended an arm to assist her walk back to her room.

During the passing weeks, my mother unraveled until it became nearly impossible to carry a normal conversation. She would speak less frequently, and her sentences became more puzzling and bizarre. Mom began to mutter odd phrases as she stared blankly. Phrases such as "Come out of there" and odder things like "Come see what I'm weaving for you in the attic." One day as I prepared her soup, she began laughing hysterically, her bulging eyes staring directly into mine as she snapped, "Why don't you crawl out of that tired old skin already?" and chills climbed my back.

The days became more worrying, but the nights became far worse. I'd hear loud, growling words being muttered through the old air vent on the wall. She began banging the walls and grumbling about larva and pupa and occasionally screaming while frantically scratching the floors from above. Whenever I'd climb the stairs to check up on her, the racing feet sounded, and I'd find her in bed, staring at me with wide, strange eyes.

This week, I woke up to see her standing in the doorway to my room with that horrible, wide grin, hyperventilating through long teeth and wide, dark eyes that both seemed disproportionately large on her face. When I asked what she was doing and flicked on the light, her face fell slack, and I heard the clanging of metal as a kitchen knife she'd been holding hit the floor. I began locking my door that night.

In the past few days, she began rocking back and forth, whispering to herself about molting and shedding, about how late I am.

That something's wrong. She stopped calling me Jack and began calling me Harvey, her father's name. She also began to chatter her teeth during the day, and at night, I heard her enamel tapping together from the vent on my wall. It sounded far too close, like she'd been directly on the other side, staring into my room.

Last night, I woke up to the sound of pounding on my bedroom door and frantic scratching. I nervously drew my curtain to reveal the barred window of my room as the scraping of a blade on the door accompanied strange shadows from the gap under it. An awful odor spilled in from the cracks, the mix of bile and decay. The clacking of teeth magnified; now a loud snapping that only stopped once she spoke in an awful, buzzing voice that carried loudly from the base of the door.

"It's time to get in the cocoon I made you, dear."

THE NEW NEIGHBORS ARE 100% HUMAN

My therapist explicitly explained that my delusional thoughts and occasional hallucinations are just manifestations of my disorder. The medication used to help, so I know it's merely paranoia eager to take the wheel again and that it seeks chaos. I knew to box away the crazy thoughts that kept popping into my head when the McKay family moved in next door, because I knew they were perfectly normal neighbors.

I knew their dog had four legs, not six. It wasn't hiding two additional thin, folding limbs under loose flaps of furry skin. I knew the bark sounded like a normal dog's, not bassy with vibratory, polyphonic overtones. I know their dog, like all dogs of course, had two eyes and not four spider-like black orbs between those floppy ears when it turned to face me.

I knew that Mrs. and Mr. McKay smiled pleasantly when greeting me. I knew their teeth were normal, not far too thin and far too many to fit inside pale white gums that stretched up high in a disturbingly wide smile. Mr. McKay's handshake was perfectly normal as well; no bones shifted under the skin to try and retain the hand's shape as I shook it. I didn't hear those crunching, squishing, and popping sounds when they greeted me in the driveway.

Their son, Tommy, was just an adorable little rascal like any other kid on the street. Kids made faces all the time, and they played jokes and messed with animals. I knew very well it was just my imagination when I looked out the window to see his jaw dislocated and hanging nearly a foot down, jiggling with unseen and impossible muscles. I saw no long needles of teeth engulfing that writhing, hissing cat before clamping down with sickening, crunching chomps.

I know neighbors borrow eggs and sugar and occasionally bring pies to the others in their cul-de-sac; it's a suburban tradition. I have no problem with that at all, and I know it's simply a matter of upping my medication and these figments will go away. I know the McKay family is perfectly normal and one hundred percent human. I just wish they'd go ring the doorbell instead of staring in at me through my second story bedroom window.

MOM NEVER LET ME LEAVE THE BASEMENT

Eight years, two months, and twenty-three days, that's how long it's been since I've been outside the basement's heavy, locked door. It sounds longer than it feels, though; days blend together down there. Every day, I read news and books and blogs. I even surf the internet for shows to watch other kids my age. I know I'll never meet them, but it helps me feel connected, and even though they can't see me, I can see them.

I've been there since I could remember, in the darkness aside from the glow of the computer's screen. I read a lot, sometimes I run around the stairs and pretend I am driving a car or flying a plane like people in videos. I never see the sky or trees, but I know what they look like, and it hurts my heart to know I'll never see them in real life.

I always wonder what they feel like; are they soft or hard? I used to think they are soft because of the way they sway from the wind.

My mom is not a bad person, despite what you might think.

She cries when she speaks to me through the gap under the door, and she slides me home-cooked meals three times a day through the tray slot, careful to look away. She sings me songs and teaches me about things outside of the basement. She tells me she wants me to be able to take care of myself when she eventually goes away, but I never know what that means.

Mom tells me dozens of times about the day she found out she was pregnant, but she never finishes the story. She tells me how my dad picked her up and began spinning her around when he found out I was in her belly. Mom explained she was unable to have kids, and she called me Milagrito, her little miracle. I love that part of the story; it always makes me feel special in a good way. I also like when she goes through the different names they came up with for me.

Barry, Arnie, Charles, Baxter (that one makes me laugh for some reason), Darryl (I hate that one), Toby, and Michael. If I was a girl, I was going to be Alice, Sarah, Penny (I like that one), Debbie, or Clara. They never got to pick, but it's fun to imagine. Mom's voice behind the door always gets shaky and sad after that part. Sometimes she stops and apologizes, and I hear her feet patter away before I hear her distant sobbing. I finally got her to tell me the whole story, though. I made her feel guilty after I lashed out for not being able to run and play outside and go to school with other kids. I made her angry, too; it was the only way she'd tell me why I was down there.

The day I was born, twelve people died. I'm sure many more people died that day, but twelve people died specifically because I was born. My mom told me how she pushed and struggled in terrible pain until finally I came out into a bright room that I almost remember. I think I remember the light and the screaming, but that's it. The doctor was the first person to die that day. Mom said he screamed until his vocal cords gave out as he started banging his head on the counter. She said he banged it on the pointy corner, over and over as hard as he could, until it made a loud cracking sound, because that was the only way he could get the image of my face out of his head.

Mom said the nurse didn't scream; she even looked calm as she reached her fingernails deep past her eyelids and plucked out her eyes.

The image was in her mind, though, so she had to keep digging deeper inside, finally using metal instruments. Dad saved my mom's life in his last moments. He threw a blanket on top of me and screamed, "Don't look at it!" over and over as he picked up the forceps and stabbed them through his temple. All the noise and commotion drew in others, though, and before I was covered up completely, the security guard saw me, unholstered his pistol, and shot his brains out. A few more nurses and patients at the hospital leaped to their deaths or slit their veins as she carried me out of there, covered in both their blood and her own.

I woke up this morning for the first time with no food at the top of the stairs, only an open door and a note. My mother had written it, explaining her heavy guilt. She wrote that today is the day she had to go away, but I saw her in her room, swaying from a rope with the breeze that bends the trees outside the windows. They're beautiful and more detailed than I imagined. I knew when I heard the scream that someone saw me from the window, and I turned when I heard the crunch as they dove under the wheels of a truck. I saw their head collapse under the tire, their only care to get rid of their memory of me.

I walked by a mirror for the first time today, and I look like nobody I've seen on the internet. I saw pictures of deformed people—burn victims and victims of flesh-eating bacteria—but none of them looked anything like me. I'm unique. I'm sorry because I know it's wrong to head out that front door, but I need to see the world. I know it's immoral and that minds and lives will be destroyed by the sight of me. I'm sorry because I know, and I don't even care.

THE KID I BABYSIT WON'T STOP EATING

My full day of summer kid-sitting began like many others, aside from the charcoal clouds that hovered low in the sky before rupturing with a brief, cool drizzle. As Mr. and Mrs. McQuaide enjoyed a much-needed extended weekend, I watched their four-year-old, Owen, a curious kid with an adorable smile and a penchant for asking me never-ending strings of questions, despite his inability to pronounce *R*s. We'd played some variant of soccer he'd invented (us kicking random balls of various sports all over the back lawn), and I was almost out of breath and ready to call it a wrap. I was beaten to it by Owen's innocent yelp after he'd fallen onto his palms on the grass. As his big, brown eyes glossed over with tears and his moan slowly rose into the wailing siren cries of a boy in pain, I realized "soccer" was finito.

I consoled Owen, asking him what was wrong, and he held out his palm, showing a round puncture wound in the meaty part of his hand near his thumb, perhaps from a thorn or stick that caught his fall in the worst possible way. "I'll help you get cleaned up, buddy," I explained and led him inside to get warm water and paper towels to clean the BB-sized wound. His small hand gushed ribbons of red, and I was worried I'd have to interrupt his parents, maybe even call a hospital, but soon the bleeding stopped and so did his tears. With a sigh of relief, I led Owen to the bathroom and sat him on the closed toilet lid as I cleaned the wound with alcohol and applied a Band-Aid. "It stopped huwting," Owen said in his sweet, high voice before framing his buck teeth in a goofy smile.

"Glad to hear it, buddy. I'm sure it'll heal soon, and you'll be as good as new in no time."

"Okay," Owen said, wiping the last of the tears from his eyes before holding his stomach with both of his small hands. "I'm huuungwy!" he said, emphasizing the word.

"No problem, kiddo. Let's make a snack!" I said enthusiastically, leading him to the kitchen, then presenting fresh deli meats and cheeses to build our own perfect sandwich. I was hungry myself, and soon we sat at the kitchen island, scarfing down mayo- and mustard-drenched snacks while watching cartoons. He chomped his down faster than me, and I cleaned the dishes as he stared with a peculiar, longing expression at the fridge.

"I'm still hungwy," Owen said, causing me to lower my head and stare at him over the lenses of my glasses.

"We literally just ate. I thought your mom said she fed you already?" I asked.

"She didn't," Owen said, looking up at me with pleading eyes.

Always a pushover, I prepared him another ham, lettuce, tomato, and cheese sandwich and watched in curiosity as he devoured it in under fifteen seconds. The boy was ravenous, and he looked a little peakish as well.

We carried on, watching cartoons until I felt nature call and excused myself to use the upstairs bathroom. When I exited the commode and began descending the stairs, I heard wrappers being crinkled. When I reached the base of the stairs and turned the corner to the kitchen, my jaw dropped.

Owen had removed a majority of the items from the fridge and was shoveling large chunks of lettuce, massive bites from blocks of cheese and, to my revulsion, what appeared to be a breast of raw chicken into his mouth. "Owen, get *out* of there!" I yelled, and he looked up at me with sorrowful eyes under high cheekbones that appeared somehow gaunt, as if he'd not eaten in a few days. "Owen, are you okay?" I asked, concerned at his behavior and sickly appearance.

"Hungwy," he said in that normally adorable voice between large bites of those raw ingredients. I walked over and picked up the scattered remains of what should have been tomorrow's lunch and perhaps dinner, trying my best to clean, but Owen's hand latched onto my wrist and squeezed, hard and bony. I felt a chill as I looked down at his hand; it was unnaturally thin with jutting bones and bulbous knuckles as if the fat and muscle had somehow been eaten away in the past hour. His face was thin with sunken cheeks, and his eyelids were inset and purple, accentuating the sharp angles of his skull. Something was very wrong.

"I'm calling your mother. I think you're sick," I told him gently, but Owen just shook his head and clawed for the remaining food before darting out of the room. "Owen!" I called, but I only heard his feet patter away. I quickly put the mess from the linoleum kitchen floor away before checking the time. Eight p.m. His parents wouldn't be home until eleven. Preferring not bother them until absolutely necessary, I headed upstairs to get Owen, as he had clearly headed into his bedroom from the direction of his footsteps. Upon arrival, I found his door was locked.

"Owen, open the door, please," I called out, twisting the knob.

"Owen, this isn't funny. Open the door," I said louder and firmly, but all I heard was wet slurping and snapping sounds from behind the wooden door. I resorted to "I'm telling your mother you were misbehaving," and soon after I heard the door unlock with a slow click. I turned the knob and pushed open the door, feeling a shiver dance up my neck at the sight of the strange, child-like figure standing in the dark room. It was Owen, but he looked absolutely emaciated, back-lit from the driveway lights as he chomped and slurped on something I couldn't quite make out in his impossibly thin arms. I flicked on the light and yelped aloud as I saw the gray fur matted with blood in his skinny arms. I knew immediately it was Penny, their cat.

I dry heaved uncontrollably from the awful smell and the sounds of snapping bone and torn flesh as he continued eating, and I stumbled backward a step into the hall, stunned by his appearance.

Owen looked somehow elderly and child-like simultaneously, his deteriorated skin wrinkled from where muscle once padded his small bones. Much of his hair had fallen out in patches, and the rest had thinned impossibly in the past hour. I then noticed his puffy hand, bruised purple and yellow and leaking black fluid in long strands onto the carpeted floor.

"Owen, I need to look at your hand," I explained as clearly and calmly as possible. He just stared at me with wide, milky-white eyes and let out a grumbling burp before continuing to chew on Penny's half-eaten corpse with giant, snapping chomps of his somehow elongated teeth. I walked slowly over, and Owen shoved the furry legs into his mouth, emphasizing the form of the bulging cat in his stretching throat as he swallowed the remains whole. Spidery veins laced over his pasty, wrinkly skin, and I swore I saw his flesh raise as something subcutaneous writhed under his neck skin and up into his cheek before wiggling under his eyeball.

"I'm still hungwy," Owen said, having engulfed the entire house cat. He then took a wobbly step on those spindly legs toward me. I stepped back, terrified well past my concern for the child as he charged toward me. I ran out of his bedroom, and he chased after, his thumping feet just behind my every step. I raced downstairs and barricaded myself in the downstairs bathroom, locking the door behind me as Owen rapidly approached. He pounded the wooden door and scratched furiously, and I actually *heard* his belly gurgling and popping with eager acids from behind the door. I watched in horror as his fingers, sickly and old, lacking any but the faintest remnant of muscle, clawed under the door, eager to get in.

I called Mr. and Mrs. McQuaide, apologizing endlessly and explaining Owen was sick and that something was terribly wrong. I waited nearly twenty minutes as those small hands pounded on the door and reached thin fingers under the gap until hearing the tires on gravel as his parents came back early to help with the situation. I heard Mr. McQuaide's voice call out "Owen?!" as jiggling keys unlocked the front door. I heard whispering as they entered, but then the voices stopped abruptly, followed by the sounds of squeaking shoes in a quick scuffle.

Eventually, I opened the door to approach the wet, crunching sounds, realizing the McQuaides were already gone. I only wished I hadn't seen that impossible, child-sized thing that was once Owen: malformed and bent with bruised, wrinkled skin wrapped over the misshapen skeleton within. Its impossibly long, bony neck stretched over a foot long to that hairless, grinning head. With bulging, cataract-white eyes, it swiveled up to face me.

I sprinted out the room and out the back door, and I didn't stop until I was likely half a mile from the house to catch my breath and call the police. I fled as my life depended on it, but not before hearing that whimper that sounded beyond desperate and impossibly famished. A soft child's voice that would stain my nightmares as it gasped for air between massive bites of its parents' flesh and gristle in order to express what was all too clear with no remorse.

"Hungwy."

I HAVE A HYGIENE PROBLEM

I brushed my teeth twice before showering as I usually do. I brushed until my stinging gums were raw and red, then I flossed until they bled, as always. I showered after that for half an hour, and I kept the water as hot as it would go. My skin flushed pink, and steam clouded the spotless, tiled space, and I scrubbed using a new loofah, plastic-wrapped and abrasive. I scrubbed hard and deep until the puffy, white skin flaked, and I stopped when it tore through and drew blood. I tended my wounds, applying gauze and medical tape to the puffy scrapes surrounded by frayed skin. I removed the brand new, folded undershirt, boxers, and socks from the sealed plastic bags they'd arrived in yesterday, and I began to dress.

I know I am obsessed with cleanliness, but I'm not here to garner criticism or phone numbers of recommended psychologists, thank you. I'm simply asking online for answers because I have a hygiene problem, and I could use help addressing it. See, I cleaned the wax from my ears as I do thrice daily, but the flashing headache I'd sustained as the cotton swab entered my ear canal was excruciating. I removed the swab, red and moist with fresh blood and what appeared to be some black detritus. It was foul and thick, almost like a paste, and it smelled absolutely terrible. It carried with it the odor of roadkill rotting in the sun, and I gasped in horror, realizing it had come from within me.

I discarded the filthy swab and fetched another, inserting it deeper within my aching ear, which popped from the throbbing pressure. I removed it and frowned down at the black residue, realizing filth had invaded my ear canal. This was, of course, the last possible place I could possibly allow bacteria to breed. I keep an array of tools to scrape dead skin and lance offending pimples. I refuse to step into a filthy hospital, of course; they are breeding grounds for sickness, contamination, and death. They try to hide the truth about MRSA, staph, and other nosocomial infections. I made a smart decision when ordering my tools last month. I opened a new, surgical steel dental pick, only intending to remove the invasive rot packed deep within my ear canal.

I wiggled the barbed pick deep within, scraping deep and far as the loud scratching and ripping vibrated the inside of my skull. I had to grit my teeth as pain hammered my temples and deeper within some place I'd not previously felt. I removed the tool, discarding the bloody pick in the bin with a clang, and I gathered a few towels to sop up the heavy flow of warm blood down my cheek and neck. I sighed, acknowledging another shower was in order once I removed the offending grime. I inserted new cotton swabs deep into the hole; they reached further now than ever, which relieved me slightly despite the fact that my hearing in my left ear seemed to be gone. I removed swab after swab of small chunks that clung to the crimson tips, mostly a pinkish grey.

I used dozens more of those swabs, digging in despite the shocking pain that shivered my body like electric shocks, and I used a new metal pick to scrape deep into the pulpy walls of my surprisingly deep ear canal, dragging it through screaming nerves. Each new swab pulled pink clumps and more jiggling morsels of filth, and I soon realized these three-inch ones were simply too short to fully reach into the deep hole I carved in order to clean the gunk out properly.

So onto my hygiene problem; I was just wondering if you guys can recommend a much longer, more rigid brand of antibacterial cotton swab from a company that does same-day shipping?

THE STRAINER

I woke up to the blaring alarm, ready to start the new job today. I peeled my face from the dried saliva sticking it to the pillow-case and trudged over to the shower, trying to get it together despite the sun being only halfway risen. I finally emerged to dress and headed to the door, nearly forgetting my coat, phone, wallet, and keys. I doubled back and fetched my stuff from the floor, rushing out to a dismal, rainy morning. I was on my way to a no-experience-needed medical assistant position, and the pay was too good to turn down.

It said very little on the Craigslist ad, just helping bedridden patients by monitoring their levels, which were listed digitally and with minimal patient interaction. No bedpans or sponge baths and only a high school diploma was needed, so I was ready to go. An hour ride on the bus flew by with the soulful sound of classics like Joe Bataan's "Ordinary Guy" through my earbuds. The heavy traffic thinned as the bus took me further from the dense city into the suburban sprawl where I got off to walk the remaining half mile.

I entered through the security gate after confirming my name on the intercom and showing my ID to the camera. Once inside, I was greeted by a very timid man in his sixties, balding and with thick glasses and a warm but awkward smile who introduced himself as Dr. Weller. He guided me to the front desk where I handed my ID over and signed in. I noticed a tear at the top of the sign-in sheet before following him back through a large hallway as he discussed my duties.

"The patients are under special care due to their very specific needs. A hospital would be far too inhumane and dangerous as we need to monitor their levels of oxygen, body temperature, and perform constant blood tests. Their looks may be shocking, but they are in less pain than they appear thanks to their medication." Dr. Weller raised his eyebrows and patted me on the shoulder as we arrived at the door to the private clinic's wing.

I was a bit surprised they opted for unskilled labor, but everything else was already taken care of digitally. I just had to make sure the machines worked, monitor the levels of the display, and return after checking the dozens of patients. I wasn't prepared for the looks of them as I stepped through the doors, swiped open by Dr. Weller's card after he handed me a stack of checklists on a clipboard and a pen. He showed me which numbers related to which value, and I only needed to catalog three values per patient. This wing of patients was separated into different rooms with doors but no windows. I entered the first room and approached the patient in bed, trying not to gawk at his shocking state.

He was bandaged from toe to head as if his skin and most of his muscle had been eaten away. Pulpy red meat secured wide eyes in the gaps of the heavily wrapped gauze that covered his entire body, and I could see by the long teeth that he had no lips and likely no face at all. I fought to maintain my composure as I approached to check the levels listed on the screen. Oxygen level 97%, BPM was 92 but soon rose to 142 after I leaned in. Respiration rate was 24, and the simple chart I'd been supplied with was now checked off and complete. I noticed the jagged, thin arms and could only wonder what butchered the poor guy before moving onto the next room.

I entered, seeing another bandaged and bedridden man who looked misshapen in some horrific accident as well. He too had wild blue eyes that scanned around the room and pierced my soul. His BPM jumped on the screen as I entered the room. It was unsettling; the man seemed clearly distressed by my presence. I saw no name or chart as they have in hospitals, which this was clearly far from. I began questioning why they didn't opt for a nurse or someone with medical experience, but the gnat of worry left when I assured myself it was because everything else was already being accounted for by the complex support system and automated monitoring. Besides, I needed the money so I kept taking down the numbers when I heard a creepy groan from the bedridden patient.

My hairs raised on my neck as a raspy tone emanated from the bandaged pulp of a man; it wasn't a word, it was like he was trying to sing but his throat had been destroyed by some unseen, corrosive horror. I began wondering if these patients were diseased, and paranoia surged throughout my mind as I began picturing a contagious, flesh-eating bacteria I was being exposed to. I backed from the bedded patient after recording his levels, figuring I'd just ask Dr. Weller a few questions before continuing. I headed back to the long hall I'd entered through but found the door locked, and panic set in.

I knocked on the door and shouted for Dr. Weller, realizing I was locked inside of this strange facility with no sign of him. I saw the cameras in the corners of the ceilings and waved to signal to him that I needed assistance. I tried my phone, finding no signal whatsoever, and I began to freak out, hyperventilating and sweating as phobias multiplied.

I pounded the door until eventually I heard the doctor over the speaker ask, "What can I help you with?"

"I just want to make sure I'm not being exposed to anything that can hurt me," I pleaded, sounding a bit more worried than I'd desired. I cursed myself for not asking this sooner, but I'm not usually the type to question an employer's methods on the first day. I fidgeted, tapping my fingertips to the thumbs of my hands, my nervous tic, until Dr. Weller finally spoke.

"I assure you these patients have nothing in any way transmittable. They are suffering from cellular degeneration, and this is not at all a threat to you." I felt a wave of relief, and with a sigh I thanked him for his answer before returning to the wing.

Time flew as I recorded heart rates and oxygen levels of the nearly identical patients. All were scrawny, horrifically injured and bandaged; all had blue eyes and all were the same height. Many of them seemed to try to signal with wide, terrified eyes or groan in tones, clearly unable to speak and likely missing tongues. I felt sorry for the men, hoping they weren't suffering, but the drip labeled Buprenorphine on their sides was likely a painkiller. I was monitoring the tenth patient when I leaned in and almost lost my balance, bracing myself on his bed and nearly touching his clearly sensitive and likely skinless leg. He let out a gasp and then fidgeted with his hands nervously. He tried to speak but clearly wasn't able, and he began softly humming a melody I'd recognized.

Joe Bataan's "Ordinary Guy" was unmistakable. I stared at the man in the bed, his terrified blue eyes the same color of my own and his bandaged, tapping fingers drumming his thumb in a nervous tic just like mine, and dread poured down over me like ice water as impossible questions sprouted in my head. I leaned in close to him, listening to his humming, and I stated my first name in introduction. The mangled, bandaged man nodded his eyes up and down as in answering "yes," and I gawked in disbelief. The man then nodded his eyes before groaning in pain from the action, but I saw them. His gold-capped molars in the back of his mouth were identical to my own. I fought my legs from collapsing as I tried to carry out the task of recording his vitals, whispering I'd try to stop whatever this was before leaving the room.

I made it through the rest of the wasted men in the beds, asking whispered questions to receive nods from their somber eyes as they all knew we were being watched. I quietly asked the remaining thirty-two identical, bedridden patients in the massive wing questions, noting each answer mentally as I wrote down their vitals.

Did you come here for a job? Yes.
Did they do this to you? Yes.
Are they going to do this to me? Yes.
Are you infected by something? No.
Are you a clone? No.
Are you me? Yes.
Did this happen your first day? Yes.
Was your first day January 12, 2018? (today's date) Yes.
Have you been here days? Yes.
Have you been here weeks? some No, some Yes.
Have you been here months? some No, some Yes.
Have you been here years? No.
Can I get out of here somehow? Yes.

I asked question after question, learning they all started just like me on this very day, as impossible and terrifying as that was. They were all versions of me, stuck in beds, some for days, weeks, and months waiting for me to show up this very day and trying to warn me of the botched experiment that sent them back in time horrifically disfigured.

The Major Harris track "Talking to Myself" looped in my manic head, unable to escape the absolute madness of the situation.

I was nearly finished with my rounds as most other versions of myself in these beds once had and knew that Dr. Weller wasn't letting me leave this facility. The last patient on my rounds knew me as well as anyone could, of course, and I asked him in desperation, "How can I get out of here?" despite knowing very well he couldn't speak. The crippled, suffering mirror of my future or past self on the bed began to hum a song I knew well, "Grateful" by Blue Magic.

Dr. Weller instructed me to just head through the "decontamination" chamber on the way out, but I was more than aware this room wasn't built for that purpose. I was about to be launched backward through time itself, a suffering vessel of skinless meat to rot on a bed like the others, but I peeked through the small window to the chamber and observed the metal grating on the floor. I braced myself, entering the chamber as the hummed tune "Grateful" looped in my head and my pulse raced as I connected the message. As the door sealed behind me, I dropped quickly to toss aside the removable floor grating and wriggled quickly within the crawlspace as the air tingled with static and the unmistakable smell of ozone flooded the space.

Dr. Weller cursed, ordering me to stop, but I was already under the chamber, approaching the hallway beyond, crawling with a flush of adrenaline that pushed me toward a white dot that became an opening in the distance. The light drew closer from above me, and I finally emerged, gazing through bandages at the drop ceiling of the place I'd just left. I was in pain despite the chemical warmth rushing into my veins from the drip at the side of the bed.

It only then clicked that the space beneath the grating was still part of the chamber that had filled with static and ozone when the machine had been activated. I'd been pulled back through the strainer effect of the metal grating, horrifically damaging my body as it was yanked through time. I had no ability to scream when I realized the consequences of my own actions were from an attempt to prevent them.

EVERY DAY I WAKE UP FARTHER AWAY

When I was a child, I would occasionally wake up standing outside of my room, confused and afraid. My mother's worried eyes would be staring into mine, her soft fingers gently gripping my shoulders. She'd explain I had been sleepwalking, and she'd spin me around with an uneasy smile and lead me back to my bed. Other times, something would wake me from my moonlit stroll and I'd realize I was standing in front of the bathroom door or in the kitchen, and I'd scurry back to bed in shame. It happened every few months: I'd sleepwalk slightly farther, and after startling my parents by standing in their bedroom doorway and talking to myself one night, they decided to take me to see someone.

After some suggestions from the psychologist, my parents began locking doors and windows, as well as limiting my stimulation before bed. No TV, no video games, and only light reading dulled the late evenings, but my episodes only seemed to become more frequent.

After they found me asleep outside on the dewy grass on the other side of the street last year, my parents were eager to find immediate help. A meeting with a referred psychiatrist led to a prescription of ProSom, a sedative and muscle relaxant tailored for cases of severe somnambulism like mine. It actually worked, although very vivid nightmares ensued.

I soon found myself locked in extremely realistic dreams of being dragged by my arm by a tall, white-skinned man who looked somehow both skinny and bloated. His bones protruded in sharp angles from his ribs and visible vertebrae. A salty ocean mist clung to him as he dragged my paralyzed legs through fields of tall wheat, the damp night air chilling my exposed skin. The man's vice-like grip ached the small bones in my wrist as he dragged me through shifting landscapes. I never got a look at his face on the other side of that lumpy head. It always faced forward, but I knew it was horrible.

I'd wake each day groggier than usual from the drug, but I woke up in my bed. Having found the solution to the troubling issue, my parents were relieved as I entered my awkward teenage years filled with hormonal spurts and the social awkwardness that accompanied them.

Each night I'd pop a chalky, bitter pill and gulp it down with water, and I would have those all-too-realistic dreams of being dragged by my arm under the starry sky. The sleepwalking had altogether stopped, however, until last weekend when I had a long overdue episode, one that changed everything.

Last weekend, my bud Jeff invited me to join him and a small group of friends to go camping up at Allegheny National Forest, and I gladly agreed. We'd made sandwiches and hiked around enjoying the fresh air before returning to the campsite. They puffed a joint while Jeff's friend Leia played the acoustic guitar in front of the licking flames of a smoky campfire. After roasting marshmallows over the orange embers, we zipped up our tents, and I soon fell asleep. I woke up six hours later to a boot prodding my chest, harder and harder, before kicking me sharply between my ribs, accompanied by a gruff voice shouting, "Get the *fuck* up!" I yelped and jolted awake, looking through bleary eyes in confusion to see a tall man in a blue uniform under long fluorescent lights. I was terrified and had absolutely no idea where I was.

I was marched by my collar through what appeared to be a shopping mall by a security guard, who accused me of hiding there during closing. Though at first eager to press charges, I think my tearful confusion threw the rent-a-cop off, and instead of calling the police, he let me call my parents if I promised never to set foot in the Warren Mall again. I blinked in disbelief when he stated the location of the small office I sat in. The Warren Mall was over an hour's drive from the campsite.

It was an eight-hour walk, an impossible achievement under any circumstance in my six-hour slumber. Rather than test the limits of the guard's patience, I nodded and complied, ringing my furious mother on the phone. Eventually, she arrived in the blue hatchback to ream me out and clarify that I was grounded. I tried to explain I had no recollection of ending up there, but the glare she gave me made it clear I was just headed for a heavier punishment. I clenched my fists and internalized my frustration as she grumbled about burned bridges and locked doors if I got a criminal record.

I stared blankly at the four barren walls of my room that evening. Despite my pleas, my mother didn't believe me. "You're not playing *that* card to weasel your way out of *this*," she snapped, and I honestly couldn't fault her. My story made absolutely no sense, yet that's exactly what had occurred. It was only the beginning, however.

That night I popped that damned pill and had that repeating, awful dream of being dragged by that emaciated man through a pasture, and he turned his head ever-so-slightly. I could make out a sliver of grotesque features, but just glimpses of them, features that belonged on no human face. I woke up screaming and drenched in sweat, lying face-first down the stairs, my sweaty head resting on the wooden floor at the bottom.

I decided to double my medication out of fear it was losing effectiveness. Two nights after, I finished off the last two pills in my prescription, and I woke on the mat near the front door of the house. I rose, exhausted and lethargic, barely able to function. I struggled through my chores that day, begging my mom for a refill of the medication, but she was too angry to reason with and suggested them being addictive with a sharp leer. Eventually she eased up and explained we could refill it later in the week.

Some creeping dread from being out of those sedatives compelled me to sleep with my jeans on, with my phone, wallet, and USB charger stuffed in my pockets. I had that recurring nightmare again, and I saw an unfeeling, black eye pivot in the socket to face me as the white hand of my abductor squeezed the bones in my forearm, dragging me through shallow swamps of cold, muddy water as crickets and frogs called out noisily into the cool night's air. I saw a sliver of a hideous, toothy smile lacking lips as the head turned slightly. The edge of that black eye peered down at my comatose, limp body being dragged. I screamed and screamed, but nothing came out.

Yesterday morning, I woke up to the irritating nibble of mosquitoes at my neck and ankles and a loud, sputtering gas-driven motor. I was lying in a grassy field surrounded by grazing horses swatting their tails at flies. It smelled of manure and fresh grass, and I shielded my eyes from the sun with my muddy hand. I stumbled through a sprawling farmland in utter confusion until spotting the source of the sound: a red-faced man with tousled gray hair and a beer belly weed whacking the tall grass. He stared at me with untrusting, squinty eyes as I approached him and asked where I was.

"Macon, Mississippi. You all right boy?" he asked with a Southern drawl.

I opened my maps and froze up in horror. He was right. I walked away quickly before the tears poured out, and I dialed my mom and listened to her shift from anger to tearful worry as I explained where I was. She apologized and made it clear she just wanted me home safe.

I was roughly a twelve-hour drive away from home, way too far to come get me, so my mom walked me through the process of getting to the airport in Jackson and boarding a plane home. She promised me that once back, she would get me immediately to the doctor's and even the police to figure out who had taken me and what was happening. She mentioned cameras and a security patrol, and she promised she'd do anything needed. My desperation faded slightly as I began the long process of trying to get back home.

The day was spent burning in the sun as I walked the two hours from the farm I woke in into town. I had in my wallet a credit card my mom gave me for emergencies, which she explained clearly that this qualified for. With her permission, I was eventually able to summon a cab, spending the entire ride on the phone. I was able to eventually reach the airport and arrange a flight that evening out of Jackson and headed to Pittsburgh. I picked up my ticket, waited through the security line, and soon after boarding the plane I was seated in an aisle seat, exhausted and radiating heat from the onset of a nasty sunburn. I hadn't even a chance to ask the attendant for a coffee, however. Try as I might to stay awake, I'd fallen asleep soon after takeoff.

Today I woke to a stick poking my cheek, held by a man with dark skin wearing a palm cowboy hat and a pale blue, button-down shirt. He was speaking so quickly that my groggy brain first didn't understand he was speaking Spanish. The man was in the process of opening his storefront on a dusty street that wound down in a steep incline. I rose to my feet with my hands up, saying, "Lo siento," the only Spanish I knew that applied. I spent the day wandering in the dry heat and found a small shop with "tarjetas, telefonicas" hand-painted on the side. My phone had no service, and it took a decent amount of time for the very friendly, older woman at the cash register to translate my questions using an app. I was in a small town called Atoyac de Álvarez, Guerrero. I watched in shock as she zoomed out on the map of her phone to show me that I was, in fact, at the bottom of Mexico.

I've been able to piece together a pattern, and I can tell I'm getting exponentially further from my home in a diagonal, Southwestern path that seems to continue on a straight line. Somehow, something is dragging me further away, and my skin crawls when picturing that horrific thing from my nightmares. Through the help of the woman at the shop, whose name is Evita, I was able to purchase a prepaid phone and call my mother, who sounded both devastated and distraught when I explained where I was. I promised I'd be all right and I would call her soon, but I had to go. I was directed to a farmacia that was able to refill my prescription by presenting the bottle, and I'm praying it will slow or temporarily halt what is happening.

At the shop earlier today, Evita let me use her map, and I was able to trace the clear, perfectly straight line that extends from Pittsburgh through Macon to Atoyac de Álvarez. The next stop based on the increase of distance in that clear direction will be near 8°S 122°W, and I just pray I can convince someone to somehow get there, though I think it will be impossible. I shoved multiple plastic bags in my pockets and will wrap my phone and wallet as well before I sleep. I have absolutely no idea what I'll find there aside from a freezing death and hungry sharks, but there is no possible way I can see myself surviving.

See, the coordinates of where I should wake up, according to the maps I repeatedly checked, are in the middle of the South Pacific Ocean...

***

Evita, the friendly older woman from the shop I'd entered, helped me with a request that pulled her friendly smile down into a puzzled, skeptical frown. With a sigh and a shake of her head, she began spouting off a long string of Spanish that sounded reprimanding, the only words I could make out being "extraño" and "equipo." She helped research my request on her phone as I used the automático (ATM), and she explained as best she could via the use of the map on both her phone and mine the location of a dive shop I'd requested, nearly three hours away. I begged and pleaded, and with a sigh, she called the shop, which would close before I'd arrive, for an urgent request. She helped arrange for the owner to wait for me to purchase a wetsuit and a lifejacket after closing hours. I thanked her immensely, handing her $60, which she tried to refuse but I insisted she take.

I purchased a few candy bars and a large bottled water, and I waited where Evita explained a communal taxi, called a "colectivo," would come by shortly. I thanked her with a clasp-handed gesture, and she mumbled something with an emphasis on the word "personaje," and I walked out into the blinding sun to wait on the side of the road for the car. I'd taken out a decent sum of money, putting the $2,500 in pesos (about $130 USD) for the equipment into my sock in case anything happened. Soon a beat-up van slowed to a halt, and I climbed over the other passengers to the free seat, explaining "Playa Las Gatas" as my destination. I was soon on my way in the bumpy van, wondering if this strange day would be my last.

I nearly nodded off on the jostling ride, but the lack of shock absorption in the beat-up van and an occasional, last-minute turn continued to jerk me awake. It stopped frequently, letting people out and in to squeeze by me as the radio played. It was easy to admire the landscape and colorful houses we passed. I realized I'd love to come back under entirely different circumstances, trying not to tear up by hoping that opportunity might exist. Eventually, we arrived, and I paid the mustached driver before jogging over to meet the tall, fit man who shook my hand, introducing himself as Pedro, in front of the scuba shop.

"Gracias, Pedro!" I said genuinely and accepted the rubbery equipment as he explained in choppy English how to use the wetsuit and fit on the life vest. I paid him the amount owed and shook his hand, feeling the adrenaline rush of the terrifying unknown waiting for me. I asked Pedro about a hotel, and he helped direct me. My arms grew tired as I hiked down the road with the heavy, neoprene suit and orange flotation vest, but I eventually arrived at a lovely building, bright orange with blue accents with a large blue swimming pool surrounded by palms.

I checked in with a bit of difficulty due to the language barrier, finally signed the receipt, and entered a clean and colorful room. I began the tedious process of organizing and waterproofing my possessions in Ziploc and plastic grocery bags. I had to stop and focus on my breathing a few times as my nerves were making every task impossible. My phone was fully charged when I dressed in the sweaty, tight scuba suit and life vest as I watched the stars emerge in the darkening purple hue of the sky. I composed a last-ditch email with the coordinates I'd deduced and sent them marked "URGENT" to my mother and friend Jeff. I explained I was stranded there and in dire need of help, and it was a matter of absolute life and death. I pressed send, praying they'd receive it then begin the complicated mess of passing on an emergency alert first thing in the morning to the coast guard, the navy, and anybody else who could possibly help reach me.

I popped two of the generic pills I'd replenished, and I blasted the AC to try and avoid boiling in the constricting wet suit. I breathed slow and steady and laid my head on the stacked pillows to compensate for my bulky, vested chest. The next thing I knew, I was in the darkness with a horrific face just out of my focal range, looming behind me, inches from mine. It was over my shoulder, teeth chattering between raspy, gurgling wheezes of watery lungs that smelled of seaweed and rot. My eyes slowly pivoted to that disfigured face, chewed of most of its rippling skin. I tried to scream, but no voice would come out, only bubbles.

I saw out of the corner of my eyes the thing that was taking me farther into the unknown against my will. Its torn flesh flapped about and danced delicately as if gravity had ceased to exist, severed veins swayed like ribbons in the wind, and white, puffy skin rippled from the butchered skull as soft currents changed direction. I looked around, seeing only a deep blue and occasional cluster of bubbles. I felt that ice-cold, bony hand squeezing my wrist powerfully until the screaming pain of a fracture jarred me alert. I then felt a downward yanking as forceful as a thousand-pound weight that tugged my arm nearly from its socket as I sank deeper and deeper down into the icy, dark water.

I awoke from the nightmare, completely submerged underwater on the ocean floor. Pain screamed in my wrist as I tried to orient myself under the deep, dark ocean as the pressure of the water squeezed my chest of precious air bubbles and panic set in. I spun frantically and nearly screamed at the hideous face of that thing from my nightmares incarnate, inches from my face with a horrific, mangled grin.

Large black eye sockets stared wide over that ghastly smile, the lips and nose nibbled off in a pulpy, red mess by fish, crabs, and other creatures. Bubbles rose from my mouth in my scream, showing me the way up as an eel slithered out from one of the eye holes. I kicked my legs with all of my strength before realizing my wrist was locked in the corpse's stiff hand. I was out of air and stuck, thirty meters down on the ocean floor, drowning.

I kicked and twisted my stuck wrist, but the pasty-white corpse's bared teeth just smiled that hideous smile mockingly as I yanked and tugged with no result. Twisting my arm seemed to loosen the corpse's waterlogged skin, and I looked down to see its legs and torso were wrapped in heavy, rusted chains, weighted down to the cloudy sediment. I felt my vision fade in black patches and realized my brain was starving for oxygen. In a downward, chopping motion, I violently shook my arm until finally feeling a lightning strike of sharp pain as my bone snapped. It was excruciating, but I was able to wiggle my flopping hand free and swim upward with the buoyancy of the life vest in the direction the bubbles had floated.

I plunged upward to breach the water's surface and breathed in a loud, starving gasp, forcefully filling my aching, air-deprived lungs.

The blinding sun flickered on the waves of the unending sea, infinite in every direction. I spun in place, afloat, and then saw the surreal sight of a white shipping container bobbing in the choppy waters, a third of it submerged below the surface.

I coughed salty water from my lungs and stared at the peculiar sight of the container not ten meters away. I floated in place for a few minutes to catch my breath and assess the damage to my wrist. It was rapidly swelling by the second, and I realized it was likely broken, just like my nightmare. The twenty-foot shipping container was the only place to go, and I paddled with my one good arm and kicking legs toward the white, rectangular box that seemed so alien in the endless sea.

I felt so small as I approached the container in the endless blue waters. I finally planted my good hand onto the metal with a *bang*. I barely had time to rejoice at surviving the horrific and impossible events when I heard a faint, feminine whimper. My eyes darted around as I realized the cries were coming from within the floating, metal box.

Soon, other high-pitched voices, scratchy from dehydration, called out in Spanish for help, and I realized multiple women were locked inside.

After struggling to climb the slippery side with a broken wrist, I spent the day on the hot, metal roof of the container, talking to the trapped women as best I could. I tried with increasing frustration to make calls or send emails to no avail with no signal. The scorching sun was relentless, beating down on my face as I tried to console them, wondering if they could understand me. I had no idea how long they had been trapped or why they were in there, but victims of sex trafficking seemed the most likely answer.

The container had likely been floating there for at least a week, since my first time waking far from home. Those poor trapped women had been sweltering in the metal prison, baking in the sun. I shivered from my uncontrollable emotions at that point, and tears cooled my sunburned face. I tried to wrap my brain around how any of this was possible and why it was happening. I played with the door, latches, but realized I might only doom them faster if the container sank, so instead I poured my bottled water into a small crack, hearing the captives rush over to drink. The stars eventually appeared in a darkening sky, and dusk brought in colder winds. It was fully dark when I eventually heard a tiny hum, growing into the distant buzz of a motor; a ship was slowly approaching.

I think part of my brain needed to make sure it was real. I cried in relief, shivering from the powerful emotions ranging from horror to happiness that washed over me like the lapping waves on the container.

It was a patrol ship painted with a French flag, sailing directly toward us. Someone must have been able to relay the message, and they miraculously had not only received it but been able to find us in the endless sea. A spotlight from the vessel locked onto the shipping container, forcing my injured hand up to block the bright beam shining onto me. I closed my eyes for an instant, but an instant was all it took, and I slipped unconscious from exhaustion.

I was standing in a freezing, white landscape, my numb fingers and face scraped by hard, arctic winds. The cold burned as my appendages lost feeling, and howling gales beat my body under rippling clothes as I stared into the distance at a bearded figure watching me. He was maybe thirty yards away, but I could see his leathery face, black from frostbite and with sunken, milky-white eyes. His lips had curled back with rot, frozen in a horrific grimace under the hood of his parka, which was stained red with streaks of frozen blood. He stood patiently in wait, biding his time as the biting breeze stirred the icicle-crusted beard on his blackened, dead face.

I gasped awake in a small hospital bed, tubes sticking into my arms with white tape. A nurse speaking in a thick, French accent soon walked over and explained I was at Ta'aone Hospital in Papeete, French Polynesia. I'd been rescued with the assistance of a Maritime Gendarmerie patrol ship who took us to the nearest medical facility.

They'd successfully retrieved not only myself, but the surviving ten of the twelve women on board that shipping container, thanks to the peculiar circumstances of my relayed distress emails and those coordinates.

The kidnapped women had been flown to Santiago, Chile, in an emergency medevac and were all expected to make a full recovery, at least physically. I was also informed the corpse of a presumably murdered sailor was recovered from the sea floor when they searched the area for other bodies, though he'd not been part of that ship's cargo or crew. I felt a cold shiver when I was told the sailor's corpse had been sunken there for about a year, as long as I'd been having those horribly realistic nightmares.

After a few days here, I'll be boarding a flight to Santiago and will then transfer to a commercial plane home to my worried family.

I've been speaking to my mother all morning over the phone, and though she's all nerves, I helped assure her that whatever is happening is over, at least for now. I'd like to think whatever dragged me across the globe had the sole intention of rescuing those suffering women in that shipping container, and that it is finished, but I can't.

I can't help but shiver in this warm bed, with lush greenery and crystal blue waters that look like paradise just outside the hospital window. I can't unsee the frostbitten face from my vivid dream last night of that frozen, bearded corpse. I can't forget the horrible grin of that solitary restless soul, standing motionless in the endless tundra.

Watching.

MY SON WON'T DIE

It was just a terrible accident, honestly a simple accident that couldn't have been avoided. I did nothing wrong to cause it. He somehow ran into the garage in that two-second span that shouldn't have happened as I backed up the truck. It was an unavoidable accident, and nothing could have prevented it, I swear to everything that exists. I didn't see him even once; I only felt the jarring thump as steel and tire connected with something that should not have been there.

I got out of the truck, ready to see a flattened basketball or a misplaced delivery Sheila is always ordering. Her stupid obsession with antiques has boxes constantly blocking the path through the kitchen and that doorbell ding-ding-dings every Saturday when I try to sleep in. I figured it was just another box until I rounded the Ford and saw the twitching little arm and the folded jaw jutting out in a bloody, vulgar angle. I dry heaved and knew he was dying; his head was bent inward, his facial features pressed into a crevice from a clearly crushed skull.

I cried, honest to God, I cried as I turned quickly away from the horrible deformation of Sean's crushed head. I only wanted to end his suffering. The damage was already done, so I got in the car and squeezed my eyes shut as tears streamed down my cheeks. I reversed the truck, hearing the crunch, and cried into the steering wheel, devastated. I sobbed and died inside, never having taken a life before.

Nothing could have prepared me for that feeling of emptiness. Nothing could have stopped my lurching terror as I heard his voice call out.

"Wha ha'n, Pah pah?" gurgling vocal chords spilled out from behind me.

"Sean?" I asked in a creaky voice, shaky from the tears. I must've imagined it. It was a bad dream was all; Sean was fine, of course. "Sean!" I shouted, sliding from the seat out the truck's door. I ran back to hug him and hold him, but I stopped dead in my tracks as I rounded the pickup and saw the standing remains of my child in the garage.

It stood upright. Feet astride, it held that mangled, folding wound of a head up on a broken neck. Dripping bits of bone and gray matter streamed down red from a pulpy hole in the center. The nose, mouth, and eyes were no longer discernible. It was a shocking mess, horrific and startling, and I yelped and stumbled back onto the concrete floor. It began dragging its feet toward me, one after another, and I screamed. It then screamed back, clearly in pain and beyond saving.

I tripped over my boots as I scrambled to the house door, bolting up the stairs to the closet in my room. I used the step stool to fetch my .45, high up and out of reach from him. I heard my wife ask what I was doing, but you can't understand the feeling of having your child mangled and suffering until it happens, until he needs to be released from that pain. Dear God, that horrible mess his head had become. Nothing could have been done to scoop the spilled brains back inside; it was beyond clear. It was just a terrible accident, and it needed to be finished.

My body shivered and tears flowed as I dragged my feet back into that garage and raised the pistol. I aimed it at that awful, crushed head that no longer held identifiable facial features, and I squeezed the grip and pulled the trigger, stinging my hand from the heavy kickback.

Red spray misted the air with a ringing bang, and nearly a pint of dark fluid splashed down to the garage floor behind it.

"Addy?" It drooled teeth and brain in blood rivers as it stepped closer to me. I squeezed off another shot, dead center, right where the brain should have once been in that mess, and the tangy gunpowder filled my dripping nostrils as I cried and screamed.

"Ah ee?" it moaned and trudged closer, a hole straight through that mush that was once my child's head. It kept approaching, and I wailed, then another high-pitched scream joined mine. It was my wife just behind me. No words could be said, only pained wailing as what was once our son walked closer and closer. I fired the remaining twelve rounds into the heart and head of the thing that was once Sean, but it didn't drop. It walked closer, oozing organs and fluids we are not meant to see, impossible and alive. My wife ran inside, and I followed, locking the door with scrambling hands.

My wife Sheila is gone now. She's a shell of rambling madness after witnessing that thing she saw in the garage that keeps pounding the door, eager to get in. She talks of devils and Satan, possession and punishment. She thinks this is hell, and I can't say I have a better answer. At some point, it broke through that door in the garage that leads to the house. We listened as that voice got louder and closer, drooling syllables thick and wet as it called to us.

Small fingers reach in under the door, wiggling digits dragging loose flesh from the bone within. Flies buzz around our room, dozens of winged spawn that cause me to flinch as I type and bat at them with shaky hands. Sheila just mumbles lullabies now, rocking back and forth in the corner, her mind gone. It's been two days, and hunger pierces my stomach. I can do nothing but stare with eyes dried from depleted tears at that skeletal paw clawing under the door as it tries to reach in, calling to me in that slow, gurgling voice: "Daddy."

THE LIKE

I tried to stay connected with family and friends after moving from Frenchtown, NJ, to Los Angeles. After four years of school and two waiting tables, I finally landed a job out there in journalism, writing for a popular culture blog. After acquiring a few thousand loyal readers, a jump in my paycheck afforded dinners out instead of the usual packet of ramen. I logged on to see the faces of my followers who got me there with the best of intentions. I posted words of encouragement for those struggling to move forward as I had, and I liked dozens of posts from family, friends, and fans to extend the positivity I felt before boarding a flight back to my hometown.

The flight was smooth but late, and I entered Newark to join the bustle of the weaving masses from the shuttle to the train as I'd done dozens of times before. I boarded in time with help of a kind gentleman as my arms were overloaded with luggage and various gifts.

My phone vibrated and dinged with alerts, as per usual, but I silenced it immediately when another passenger shushed me and pointed to the sign reading "quiet car." I eventually finished reading the paperback I'd started on my flight. The sky dimmed to black before my station was announced. When I finally opened my phone, I realized something was wrong.

There were hundreds of missed calls, emails, and texts. I scrolled through them with a spreading nausea as new ones kept spewing forth. I was being called filth, scum, trash, evil, and much worse. I kept skimming through in confused tears. My employer had fired me via email, and I was blacklisted, my roommate wanted me out, even my parents suggested a hotel for the night. My name was trending on every media outlet, the viral news on network television. I opened links to the breaking story about me, "Blogger Mocks Grief-Stricken Family." My photo was next to my "like," a laughing emoji my hand slipped to when "liking" the post, with millions of views and no apology.

The child was named Stephanie; she'd been bullied horribly before her body washed up near the bridge. I recognized the sweet, smiling face I had meant to "like" but accidentally clicked "laugh" on. I breathed deep in thought. I could explain this whole ordeal in time. I wiped my tears and exited the train shaking, but then I noticed that photo I was tagged in. A Bowie knife with myself in the background reading on the train. I looked up to the dark, empty platform of the station as the train pulled away, noticing the man who'd helped me earlier blocking the stairs, glancing at his phone then back at me. I looked at my screen and read the caption underneath, "10,000 likes and I'll do it." As the number beneath ticked past 9,999, I heard the fast thumping of boots getting louder.

MY DOG STOPPED EATING

I first stared at Mable's bowl of untouched food with concern, wondering if she might be sick. I found her slumped on the carpet, a sad look in her eyes that my lab-pit mix rarely expressed. Usually she'd pant and lick my face or dart through the house full of zoomies, but something was different. I petted her velvety head and called her a good girl, but she just looked so defeated. That evening, I plopped another helping of food in her dish next to the untouched one, but she ignored it.

I took to the internet to find answers, and my worries only flourished.

Dog depression is indeed a thing, as are dozens of terrible ailments and parasites, possibilities that filled me with concern. I finally closed the laptop and drove to Petco to pick up some organic options, wet and dry selections in salmon and chicken; I even bought lox and eggs in case all else failed. It did. Mable just stared at me with a sad gaze; even the sizzling bacon was left untouched. I made an appointment with the vet on the phone and tried to comfort her as the hours led in the night, and I eventually slipped in the sheets to sleep.

My nightmare was far too real, the pain far too real as those jagged teeth sawed into my flesh. Those deep, violent growls shook me as my torn arms streamed red with blood. I woke up screaming to see her face. Mable was standing over me, staring down at me from above. I called her name, but she just loomed over me for a good minute before licking her chops, jumping off the bed, and leaving the room. I was unnerved but eventually fell back asleep.

The next day she didn't touch her food, and that night I again had that horrible dream of my body being ripped apart by Mable's sharp teeth. I woke again in panic and drenched in sweat to the face of my dog staring down at me. I yelled at her, commanding her out of the room, and she just licked her jowls and glared at me before I pushed her out. I closed my door last night for the first time.

Today I woke up from that same nightmare, her sharp teeth and my chipping bones, and I screamed out, bolting upright in the stained bed, now damp with the red spatter of blood. I panicked, searching my body for wounds. A ripping sound drew my attention to the floor, to Mable's blood-stained mouth feasting on the body of a large man wearing a shredded black tracksuit. He must have broken in through my bedroom window, his hands clenching a long buck knife and a crowbar, his still face twisted in a horrible grimace. "Good girl," I called out, and dialed 911 as I watched her finally eat, filled with both horror and awe…

THE DELUSION OF FREE WILL

I was out drinking with coworkers at a bar in Midtown, enjoying a night of excess, until one by one we parted ways as we all had work in the morning. I remember staggering toward the train and that man in a blue poncho who seemed to be following me. I remember being anxious and quickening my pace. I remember him closing in and running before I fell hard to the pavement. When I woke up, I was in a dark chamber with brushed metal walls over four meters high. My head pounded in my skull, and I had no idea where I was.

"Who we are is not important. You have become a vital component of an experiment in order to help us maximize our capabilities. The room you are now in branches off into two distinct pathways. One path will lead to the exit, and you will be free to leave.

"The other will provide a horribly painful demise. The walls in this chamber will heat until you cook to death if you choose neither. That's it. You're free to go. Most of the others chose the left passage. Goodbye and good luck."

I sat on the damp ground, trying to comprehend what was happening and why. I gazed into the black velvet shadows that inhibited even the slightest glimpse of what lay ahead and then felt the vibration as a current was switched on and warmth began to emanate from the metal walls. I begged for mercy and cried to the speakers. I slammed my fists on the tall, steel wall that hissed as the water droplets shrank and steamed from the surface. I was being baked alive and edged closer to the barely visible passageways.

My mind raced frantically to solve my survival. The voice had mentioned that most take the left, but he was clearly trying to manipulate me. This seemed like some mind game to me, and I rationalized he was trying to get me to oppose his suggestion and take the right in rejection of his notion. But he knew I'd make that decision, so I should choose left, he suggested as if to fake me out two moves ahead, clearly.

The heat rippled the air and my jeans and shirt felt like a hot iron where they touched my skin as I frantically thought. He knew I'd choose right, then left in defiance, so then the right path must be it. I ran from the singing heat that seared my flesh, knowing I had solved it. I glimpsed a shadow to my right as I sprinted in before the floor collapsed. I fell for meters, then slammed onto sharp spikes that punctured through my chest and legs with intense pain.

"And that's the delusion of free will," the voice explained to someone unseen as my stinging body bled out. "Nobody sees the third passage if we tell them there are two."

MY CHILD'S FIRST WORDS WERE NOT MAMA

Charlie was born a tiny pink, wiggling ball of screams. He was a month premature, dashing out as if he had places to go and people to see. My wife joked that he had the voice of an angel; his harsh screams could strip paint from walls and fine hairs from inner ears. Beth and I took turns so that one of us could actually get some sleep in the basement on occasion. As the grueling months passed and bags formed under our eyes, we realized we were in it for a longer haul than we'd imagined.

At six months, Charlie was still as loud as ever, though a bit more charming with that shiny wave of black hair. He seemed to calm a bit when I'd read to him, so we ended up reading entire novels to our little, vocal angel. He hated breastfeeding and preferred the bottle, something we both found odd but accepted after speaking to our pediatrician. Charlie was otherwise healthy, and we were advised to just hang in there through his shrill fits. Advil and noise-blocking earmuffs became regularly used tools in our arsenal.

When Charlie reached twelve months, we grew concerned and took him to an infant psychiatrist to cover the bases. We had ruled out anything physical, but his streaming wide eyes and drooling, screeching mouth seemed to harbor something deeper that we felt we needed to explore. The doc mentioned emotional regulation disorder as a possible cause and suggested we perform certain playful interactions, imitating Charlie until he recognized our mimicking behavior and played along in sucking a thumb or laughing. We continued to try, but nothing worked.

It wasn't until a few months after his birthday, when Beth was in the bathroom, that Charlie finally spoke.

I'd been playfully crawling on the carpet to copy his behavior when Charlie sat up and stared at me with trembling, glossy eyes, pointing a nubby little finger to the closed bathroom door. A tickle of unease danced across the hairs on my neck as he scrunched his face into a tearful pout and spoke his first words. "Not mama," he whimpered, shaking his tiny head "no" as tears streamed down his tender, pink face.

I swung my head over to the bathroom, staring at the silhouette of Beth standing strangely in the doorway with her hair up. I then noticed the stapled seam reflected in the mirror that ran down the back of her head for the very first time.

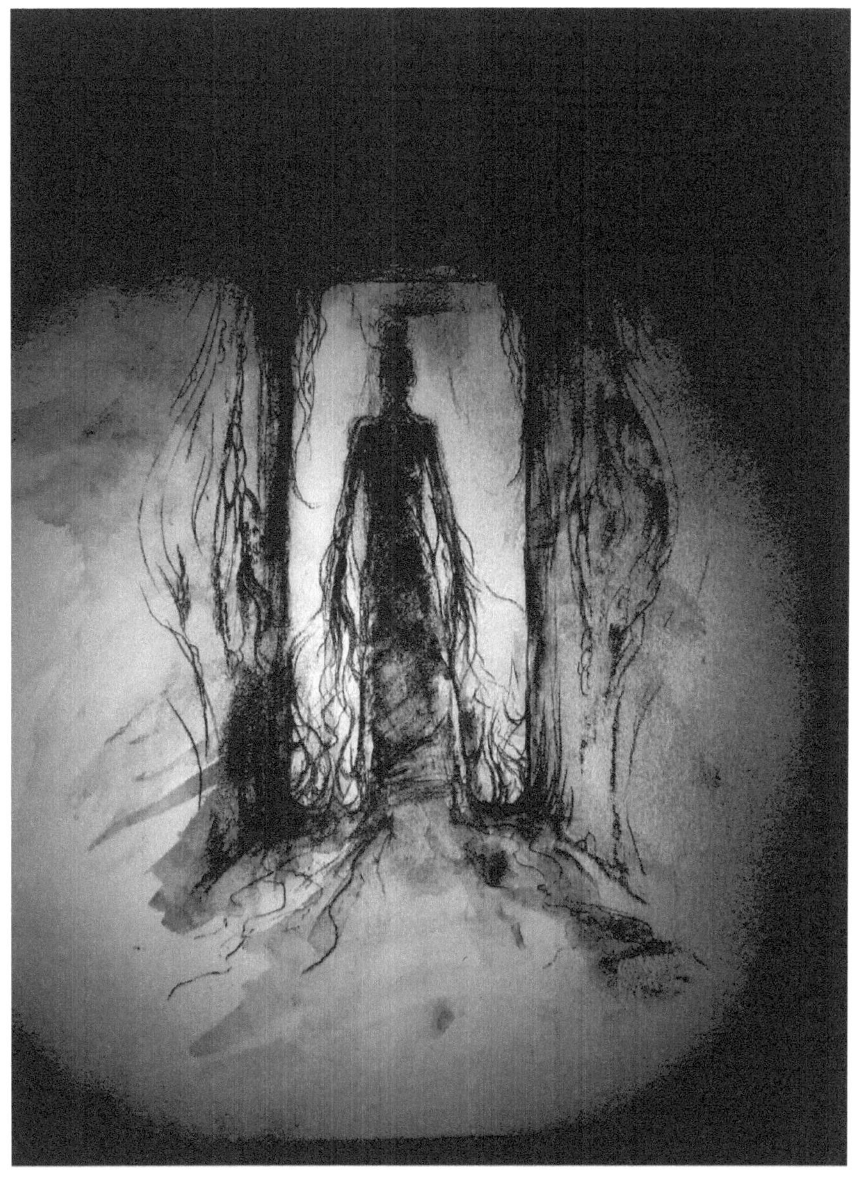

THE SCARIEST RIDE IN THE WORLD

The buttery smell of popcorn, joyful calliope melodies, and the thrilled screams of children filled the air. The summer state fair had once again sprouted dusty canvas tents, junk food carts, and bulb-speckled rides. In the back, the self-proclaimed "Scariest Ride in the World" kept most sugar-sticky kids at bay, but not Seth.

Seth smirked at the haunted house ride, festooned with carved and painted skulls, serpents and spiders. He puffed his chest, then marched through the mouth-shaped entrance, unafraid.

His eyes fought to adjust to the darkness, and he nearly yelped at the sight of the decrepit ticket taker extending an open palm. Seth grumbled as he fished for a ticket and placed it into the wrinkled hand. The grinning old man pointed a bony finger to the solitary cart sitting on the track. Seth approached and slid into the wooden seat, and the rickety cart clacked along the track into the darkness ahead.

The cart rattled on the rails past dusty animatronic dummies, a cackling witch to his left, a shoddy ghoul to his right.

A laughable rubber ghost charged on a zip-line and a jiggling rubber spider straight out of a Halloween supply store dropped and dangled above him. "Scary, my ass," Seth huffed, then spat a loogie onto a cheap plastic skeleton. Bored, he stood up and hopped from the slow-moving cart onto the floor beside the track.

He began to kick at the motorized ghouls and stuffed black cats. He even unzipped his jeans and pissed inside a shadowy alcove, nearly yelping when a surprisingly realistic bat flapped out from within, nicking his forehead. Ignoring the sting, he chuckled as he kicked over plastic gravestones and yanked fake cobwebs down from the ceiling. Seth laughed as he strolled back outside onto the sunlit fairground.

In the following days, Seth bragged to his peers about his exploits on the childish ride. He neglected the two tiny red dots on his forehead, which began to tingle and itch. A week passed before Seth fell ill with what seemed like the common flu. Days later, an intense feeling of dread haunted his every waking moment, and he writhed in constant agitation. By the time he'd confessed about how he'd gotten the tiny bite, the rabies virus had penetrated his brain.

Seth would soon be unable to drink water, violently coughing it from his stinging throat. Hallucinations more horrific than his darkest nightmares would torment him daily. Spasmodic contractions would ripple through his aching muscles as he lay strapped to a hospital bed, foaming at the mouth. Seth would tremble and moan in absolute agony in those long days before his certain death. But that relief would come much later, for the scariest ride in the world had only just begun.

MORE CHILLS FROM VELOX BOOKS

MORE CHILLS FROM VELOX BOOKS